PRAISE FOR *JOHN AND MARY MARGARET*

"What if at least some of our life decisions do come with second chances? Susan Cushman answers this question through the late-in-life romance of John and Mary Margaret, and a rediscovered love never realized in their youth. Filled with the sights, sounds, and flavors of Mississippi, Cushman's story opens a heartfelt and authentic window not only into two lives, but into the South then and now."

—**Lisa Wingate**, #1 *New York Times* Bestselling author

"Frederick Douglass may have been right when he wrote 'the white and colored people of this country [can] be blended into a common nationality, and enjoy together . . . the inestimable blessings of life, liberty and the pursuit of happiness.' Susan Cushman's *John and Mary Margaret* is written in the spirit of Douglass's vision. Set against the backdrop of the University of Mississippi in the mid-1960s, this clear-eyed book confronts the historical and social realities of those times and the once perilous nature of interracial intimacy."

—**Ralph Eubanks**, author of *Ever Is a Long Time* and *A Place Like Mississippi*

"Susan Cushman has captured the heart and soul of the Old and New South with her powerful literary saga. Spanning five decades of two star-crossed lovers' courageous and perilous journeys in Mississippi and Memphis, *John and Mary Margaret* conveys the power of love to overcome historic racial injustice. I can't stop thinking about it!"

—**Lisa Patton**, bestselling author of *Rush* and *Whistlin' Dixie in a Nor'easter*

"Susan Cushman's *John and Mary Margaret* is an elegantly written and beautifully understated love story. Two young people from adjacent, yet distant worlds, fall in love only to find the cultural space in which they discover each other is not comfortable with or accepting of their relationship. But decades later, Cushman gives that love a second chance, and we are truly lucky to bear witness to her notion that true love might be delayed but it will never be fully denied."

—**Jeffrey Blount**, author of *The Emancipation of Evan Walls*

"With great sensitivity, author Susan Cushman balances themes of duty with racial upheaval in the changing times of the Deep South. Thought-provoking, engaging, and ultimately hopeful, *John and Mary Margaret* is an insightful, heart-warming story of the perils of love in historically pivotal times."

—**Claire Fullerton**, multi-award-winning author of four novels and one novella

"With sweetness and grace, Susan Cushman brings John and Mary Margaret's story to life. Sometimes true love can be complicated, especially in the south during the 1960s. But John and Mary Margaret have a story to tell, and Adele Covington—from Cushman's debut short story collection, *Friends of the Library*—knows it's going to be a good one. She's right, of course, and this *is* a love story in more ways than one. Susan does a beautiful job weaving everyone's story together for an ending that makes you want to jump for joy."

—**Mandy Haynes**, author of *Walking the Wrong Way Home*

"This sensitive and well-written work of historical fiction explores the deleterious impact of racism on our basic human relationship. Luckily, sometimes we get a second chance."

—**Eileen Harrison Sanchez**, author *Freedom Lessons*

John and Mary Margaret

by Susan Cushman

ISBN 978-1-64663-390-6

REVIEW COPY: This is an advanced printing subject to corrections and revisions.

Published by

köehlerbooks™

3705 Shore Drive
Virginia Beach, VA 23455
800-435-4811
www.koehlerbooks.com

JOHN *and* MARY MARGARET

A NOVEL

with much love,
Susan

SUSAN CUSHMAN

VIRGINIA BEACH
CAPE CHARLES

DEDICATION

For my granddaughters:

Grace, Anna, Gabby, and Izzy.

May the world embrace you with

love and kindness.

"The writing of a novel is taking life as it already exists. What distinguishes it above all from the raw material, and what distinguishes it from journalism, is that inherent is the possibility of a shared act of the imagination between its writer and its reader. There is absolutely everything in great fiction but a clear answer."

—Eudora Welty

"Not everything that is faced can be changed, but nothing can be changed until it is faced."

—James Baldwin, *The Cross of Redemption: Uncollected Writings*

"Each time a person reaches across caste and makes a connection, it helps to break the back of caste."

—Isabel Wilkerson, *Caste*

"I am leaving this legacy to all of you . . . to bring peace, justice, equality, love and a fulfillment of what our lives should be."

—Rosa Parks

TABLE OF CONTENTS

Great fiction shows us not how to conduct our behavior but how to feel. Eventually, it may show us how to face our feelings and face our actions and to have new inklings about what they mean. A good novel of any year can initiate us into our own new experience.

—Eudora Welty

CHAPTER 1

Book Club (2015)

John wasn't the first man to join Mary Margaret's book club in Harbor Town, the scenic neighborhood on Mud Island in downtown Memphis developed in 1989. The club had never been one of those women's groups that were mainly into beach reads and chick lit. The members' monthly selections were as diverse as the members themselves. Retired physicians, lawyers, and architects read alongside younger career types, and their choices ran from Southern, literary fiction and historical fiction, and John Grisham legal thrillers to scholarly biographies, weighty political tomes, and celebrity memoirs. No, John wasn't the first man in the club. He wasn't even the first Black man. But he and Mary Margaret were the group's first biracial couple.

They cut a fine figure as they walked around Harbor Town, often on their way to nearby Café Eclectic for morning coffee and scones, or to Tug's restaurant for an early dinner on the patio, arriving back home in time to watch sunset on the Mississippi River from their front porch or balcony. River Park Drive, like so many streets in the New Urban neighborhood, was lined with candy-colored traditional homes with front porches that encouraged community. Garages were hidden behind the houses, and walking was more common than driving.

John Abbott was seventy-two. His mostly gray hair was cropped short. He often wore a light denim shirt, a houndstooth sports jacket, and starched jeans, which usually topped off a pair of cowboy boots. He was six-foot-two and carried himself with dignity, with a physique and posture that had served him well during his years as an attorney in Memphis, and later as a judge. Tortoise-shell glasses framed his intense dark eyes, which seemed to find their way to a view of Mary Margaret as often as possible.

Mary Margaret's slim figure, which she maintained with yoga and daily workouts at the gym, was often adorned with black slacks and an Eileen Fisher sweater set, sometimes in winter white or pastel blue or pink. A blonde when she was younger, her hair was darker now with a touch of silver, and she usually wore it pulled back into a low, messy side bun. Beautiful diamond studs and a matching tennis bracelet were her favorite jewelry. When she and John went out, she usually carried a leather Coach cross-body clutch that moved gracefully on her right hip as she walked. Tonight, the book club was meeting at a neighbor's house just around the corner. Mary Margaret was especially excited because the club was going to have a visiting author.

A couple of weeks earlier, Mary Margaret had received an email queueing up the book-club jam session. She had set down her coffee cup and looked over the top of her laptop at John, who was buried in the morning paper.

"John?"

"Yes?" he answered, without looking up.

"Have you checked your email today?"

"I've barely finished my first cup of coffee and haven't even gotten to the sports page of the paper yet. I thought we were supposed to be retired. What's the hurry to read emails?"

"Well, this just caught my eye. It's from Sharon, with the book club."

"So, we already know which book we're reading this month. What does she say?" John put the paper down and headed to the kitchen counter to refill his coffee cup.

"She says that the author of the memoir we're reading has agreed to meet with our group. She's the woman who wrote about caring for her mother who died from Alzheimer's, remember?"

John turned and faced Mary Margaret. "Oh, that's a nice surprise. The author lives in Harbor Town, right?"

"Yes, and she's friends with Sharon, and it's Sharon's turn to host the meeting. Won't it be good to talk with her in person, about her journey with her mother?"

"I'm sure it will be." He leaned down and gave her a kiss on the cheek.

The day of book club meeting came during a crisis for John and Mary Margaret.

"How is he?" John asked, as Mary Margaret hung up the phone.

"Well, he did it again. He pulled his feeding tube loose from his abdomen, and they are taking him back to the emergency room to reinsert it."

"Why can't they keep him from doing that?" John asked. "Don't they have layers of bandages over the site so he can't touch it?"

"Of course they do, but they can't watch him every minute, and sometimes he finds it when he's in bed, which is what happened early this morning."

"Do we need to go to the hospital?"

"No, they will take him for the procedure and then take him back to the nursing home later. We can go check on him tomorrow morning."

As they arrived at Sharon's house, members were gathering for refreshments, and eventually the living room filled with around twenty people. Sharon introduced the visiting author.

"Welcome, everyone. We are so happy to have a local author and Harbor Town neighbor with us to discuss her book tonight, which we've chosen as our book of the month. Adele Covington will be talking with us about her memoir, *A Mother and Daughter Face Alzheimer's.* Adele grew up in Jackson, Mississippi, where most of the book is set. Adele, please tell us what prompted you to write this book."

"Hello, everyone, and thanks so much for inviting me. It's great to see so many neighbors I already know, and to meet new ones. My mother died from Alzheimer's in May of 2016. I never actually took care of her in my home—or hers—since she was in a nursing home in Jackson for the last eight years of her life. I made the four-hundred-mile round trip from Memphis to visit her once or twice a month during the years she was in the nursing home. And yes, the emotional and spiritual aspects of being a caregiver are different than the physical responsibilities, but they can take a toll."

Mary Margaret noticed several attendees nodding as Adele spoke, and she stole a glance at John, who gave her a slight smile.

"My father died in 1998, and when my mother started showing signs of dementia a few years later, I sold her house and moved her into an assisted-living facility. Once she adjusted, she was happy there for about three years. But then she broke her hip, and after a few days in the hospital for surgery and a few weeks in a nursing home for rehab, it became clear that she could never return to assisted living. She entered a different nursing home in 2008, ten years after my father's death. We didn't know she would live another eight years, enduring a slow and awful decline as the tangles and plaques took over her brain cells."

Sharon asked a question as Adele paused to take a sip of water. "Tell us why you decided to write a memoir. And what was that process like? It seems like the long-distance caregiving would have been physically and emotionally difficult enough, without taking time to write a book about it."

"Well, it was an interesting process," Adele began. "For one thing, I have a blog, and during the last eight years of my mother's life, I wrote over sixty blog posts about my visits with her, our relationship, and the stages of her decline. Some of the readers of the blog suggested that I turn those posts into a book, so that's what I did. I just organized the posts into a single manuscript, wrote an introduction, and found a small press to publish it. In some ways it was the easiest book I've written, but the hardest one I've lived."

Mary Margaret reached for John's hand and squeezed it lightly. He squeezed back and gave her a quick nod.

"So, have you written other books, Adele?" one of the book club members asked.

"Yes, I've published a novel and a short story collection, and edited a couple of published anthologies of essays." She paused for a moment and then asked the group, "Are any of you currently taking care of anyone with Alzheimer's or dementia, or have you done this in the past?"

A few people raised their hands, including Mary Margaret and John. When he put his hand down, John solemnly stared at the floor. Mary Margaret patted his hand and smiled gently at him, but he didn't look up.

Adele engaged the group with a discussion about the various stages she had described in her book—her mother's transition from independent living to assisted living to nursing home care, and the accompanying physical and emotional struggles that came with each of these. They talked together about the difficulty of letting go, and especially how painful it was when the loved one no longer recognized the family members. A few people in the group shared their personal stories, but John and Mary Margaret remained quiet. After the meeting, Adele approached them.

"Hi. I noticed that you raised your hands, indicating that you might be taking care of someone with dementia or Alzheimer's, but you didn't share any of that with the group. I hope I didn't say anything that made you feel uncomfortable."

"Oh, no, not at all," Mary Margaret answered. "It's just that my story—well, our stories—are a little complicated. Not really something we'd want to share with a group."

"Oh, I'm so sorry if I overstepped," Adele looked apologetically at both of them. John remained quiet and looked away towards a window.

"It's okay," Mary Margaret offered. "We wouldn't mind talking about it privately, but we're not sure who to talk with. I know you're a super-busy author on a book tour, but do you know someone here in Memphis you could recommend for us?"

"You mean, like an elder-care counselor?" Adele asked.

"I guess so. I haven't really thought about it."

"I'm not sure we really need that," John said, looking at Mary Margaret when he spoke. "I think we've got everything under control."

"Oh, I'm sure you do," Adele said. "But sometimes it helps just to share your story with someone else who has been through it—even if the details aren't exactly the same."

John raised his eyebrows and shrugged. "Oh, I'm sure the details aren't the same."

Mary Margaret started slowly, looking at John and then back at Adele. "Maybe you could come by our house for a visit and a light lunch one day soon? We live right around the corner from Sharon. Our house faces the river."

John appeared surprised by the invitation but then nodded his consent. Adele smiled as she answered, "Oh, I would love to."

"We're busy tomorrow, but how about Thursday? Around noon?" Mary Margaret asked.

"That sounds perfect. Here, my number is on this card. Just text me your exact address and I'll be there."

Walking from her home to Mary Margaret's on Thursday, Adele passed several ducks that were crossing a small bridge from one pond to another. She admired the view of the Mississippi River as she turned north on River Park Drive—a route she often took at sunset. In a few minutes she was at Mary Margaret's house, a stately, pale green, two-story foursquare with a wide front porch covered by a balcony. The small front yard was beautifully landscaped and the porch had large pots filled with green and red caladiums.

John greeted her at the door and escorted her into the kitchen where Mary Margaret was making coffee and setting out a pitcher of lemonade and a plate of egg salad sandwiches. They moved comfortably around each other—like a couple that had been together for many years—and the three of them sat at the breakfast table when the coffee was done. After a few quiet moments, Adele broke the silence.

"So, you didn't share any of your stories at the meeting. I'm very interested to know more about your situation. Do either—or both of you—have a parent with Alzheimer's?"

Mary Margaret answered, "Neither. In fact, all four of our parents are dead."

"Oh, I'm so sorry. I just assumed—"

"It's a long story, Adele. I guess I'll begin at the beginning. You see, John and I were sweethearts at Ole Miss, back in the 1960s."

"We were there just a couple of years after James Meredith became the first African American admitted as a student," John added.

"Yes, we were both freshmen in 1966." Mary Margaret said.

Adele asked, "How did you decide to go to Ole Miss at such a difficult time, with so much racial unrest, John?"

"Maybe you should tell her about your childhood or at least your high school years in Memphis first," Mary Margaret suggested.

John set his coffee down on the table, leaned back in his chair, and clasped his hands together, as if he was quietly preparing for one of the many legal presentations he had given during his career. His mind traveled back to his childhood. His father's dreams for him. And his own dreams.

The world of most men is given to them by their culture.

—Richard Wright, *The Outsider*

CHAPTER 2

John (1960s)

John grew up in an all-Black neighborhood in Memphis, in the 1950s and 60s. His father, Richard Abbott, was a football coach at the school John attended from ninth through twelfth grades. His mother, Dorothy, was a seamstress who worked from home and did custom ball gowns and alterations, mostly for the Midtown society ladies and their daughters. And his older brother, Frank, was a natural athlete and a star on the high school football team their father coached. Richard pushed John to follow in Frank's footsteps, although John preferred to spend his after-school hours at the library. At a young age he watched the movie, *Witness for the Prosecution,* and he loved to watch *Perry Mason* and *The Defenders* on television, but his real love was reading. *The Reivers* was published in 1962, when John was only fourteen. Of course he had no way of knowing it would be the last book William Faulkner would write, or that it would win the Pulitzer Prize the following year. He just loved the characters. He checked it out over and over at the Cossitt Library downtown. Memphis libraries had only been desegregated in 1960, and John was one of only a few Black kids who frequently used the previously all-White library, which he preferred to the *Negro branch libraries* around Memphis.

One afternoon in the library, he lost track of the time while reading. It was getting dark outside and his mother always warned him about not being downtown too late in the afternoon. Walking out the door onto Front Street, he immediately noticed a group of older White teenagers hanging out at the corner. They saw him, too, and began walking towards him. His bike was on a rack between him and the boys, so he had no choice but to walk towards the bike rack and hope that the boys wouldn't harass him. He nodded in their direction, as if they were his friends, carrying himself confidently and unrushed. As soon as he pulled his bike from the rack one of them shouted, "Hey, nigger! What do you think you're doing in our library?"

Losing his confidence from a minute earlier, he jumped on his bike and pedaled furiously away just as another boy shouted, "You better not have gotten your cooties all over our books!"

This was something John had not yet experienced in his young life, and it wouldn't be the last time. It would be years before realizing his dream of becoming a lawyer. Meanwhile, he needed a way to defend himself. Maybe his father's insistence that he play football wasn't such a bad idea after all. He was tall for his age and the next couple of years would add some bulk to his slim frame, so he began playing in ninth grade.

His father had big dreams for both of his sons to play college ball at the historically Black Tennessee State University (TSU) in Nashville. But a different dream had been growing in John's heart since October of 1962 when James Meredith became the first African American to be admitted to the University of Mississippi. John was only in eighth grade at the time, but Meredith's courage inspired him. It would take a few more years for John to be brave enough to face his father with his dreams.

After Frank graduated high school and went on to play for TSU,

John was a senior and he stepped into his brother's position as star quarterback. He took his team to a winning season, and the letters started coming in from TSU and other historically Black colleges, recruiting him. But John wanted a change—the chance to be part of the change so badly needed in the South. Behind his father's back, he applied for admission to the University of Mississippi (almost universally referred to as "Ole Miss") and waited quietly for a reply. Meanwhile, he had a new distraction—girls were after him. Tall and handsome and mysteriously shy, he was considered a real catch by most of the females in his school.

His first date was really just an afternoon outing with Jacqueline Price, a popular cheerleader in John's class. Tuesday was the only day that Blacks were allowed entrance at the Memphis Zoo, so it was a popular day for after-school outings for kids like John, especially during the spring. After an hour walking around the various exhibits, the couple grabbed some popcorn and settled down on a bench. John looked at his watch and then at Jacqueline.

"We probably shouldn't stay too long, with exams coming up, you know?"

"Oh, they don't start until next week, John. We've got plenty of time. I usually wait until the day before each test and try to memorize as many facts as possible so I won't forget them."

"What about literature? It's about so much more than just memorizing facts."

"Yeah, I don't really like to read, so I usually just scan the *Cliffs Notes* and hope the teacher asks questions from them."

"You don't like to read? Not even for pleasure?"

Jacqueline shook her head as she took another handful of popcorn.

"How do you expect to learn more about culture and politics and things that impact our lives? Haven't you even read *The Fire Next Time* by James Baldwin?"

"What?" Jacqueline panicked. "Is that going to be on our lit exam? I've never heard of it."

John couldn't believe his ears. "You know who James Baldwin is, right?"

"Well, not really. Some poet or politician, or what?"

"He is just one of the most important Civil Rights spokesmen of our time," John began. "He writes about racism and religion, and what's happening to Black men in America."

"Oh, well, that's why I haven't read it, since I'm not a Black man," Jacqueline joked. "Oh, look! There's Betty and George." She hopped up and ran to greet her best friend who was looking at the giraffes with her boyfriend. John sighed, shrugged, and slowly moved to join them.

Even with their intellectual and literary disconnect, John and Jacqueline continued to date for the rest of their senior year. Jacqueline was a pretty hard habit to quit, with her long curly eyelashes, which she flaunted, and her irresistibly kissable lips. Not to mention that body—toned from years of cheerleader practice and running track.

Blacks were only allowed to sit in the balcony at the movie theaters, a choice spot where couples made out, so that's where John and Jacqueline often ended up on Saturday nights. On one of those nights, they were double-dating with another couple. Denise was on the cheerleading squad with Jacqueline, who had gotten her a date with her cousin James, who went to another school. James was small for a seventeen-year-old, but he and John were kindred spirits because they both loved books. As they were leaving the theater, two White couples were walking out the doors just ahead of them. As the last boy in the group looked over his shoulder to hold the door for them, he quickly let it close in their faces. John bristled when he heard laughter on the other side of the door.

"Leave it alone, John," Jacqueline said, knowing that John's sense of civil justice could get him in trouble.

But as John held the door for Jacqueline and James and Denise and followed them out of the theater, the White couples were waiting for them. One of the antagonistic boys jumped on James, who was no match for his physical size or strength. The other White instigator was yelling, "That'll teach 'em where they belong!" But just as the first boy was about to land another punch on James' face, he looked up and saw John, towering over him at six-feet-two with shoulders to match, and bulging muscles from years of football practice and hours in the gym.

"What did you say?" John asked as he pulled the White boy off James.

"So, what are you, his bodyguard or something?"

Just as John was getting ready to punch him Jacqueline grabbed his arm, and Denise ran to help James, who was on the ground, bleeding from his mouth and nose. "Come on, John. You can't teach them anything with violence."

Those words, unusually serious and poignant for Jacqueline, reminded John of his dream. Someday he would be able to protect his people in the courtroom, or maybe by changing laws to make life better for his race.

As the spring of 1966 wound down, John and Jacqueline prepared for senior prom. It was all John's mother could talk about for weeks, not only because she was so happy that John and Jacqueline were going, but also because of how busy she was sewing and altering prom dresses for many of the senior girls.

"I can't wait to see you and Jacqueline! Now you be sure and bring her by the house so I can take a picture of y'all all dressed up. Have you got her corsage, John?"

"Yes, Mama. I got one with those with little tiny roses on it, just like you told me."

"She's going to love it."

On prom day, John and his best friend, George, picked up their dates—George was with Betty, his steady girlfriend since tenth grade—and headed to the school gymnasium. Jacqueline looked beautiful in her yellow chiffon dress and white high heels, and once they arrived at the dance all she could talk about was what everyone else was wearing. Or who they were with. She shunned invitations to dance with other boys, clinging to John all night like a prized trophy. When the disc jockey played Wilson Pickett's "Land of 1,000 Dances," a crowd gathered around Jacqueline and John, who had become the center of attention. Jacqueline sparkled, and John tried to enjoy the moment. But his mind was elsewhere. For him, the prom was just another reminder that high school was ending, and decisions about his plans for college consumed his every thought.

John and Jacqueline met at The Pig 'n Whistle the following Tuesday afternoon, and of course all Jacqueline's friends were there. They huddled around the booth where the popular couple were seated, gossiping with Jacqueline and flirting with John. Finally, Jacqueline's friends wandered off, and the two were alone with their barbeque and Cokes. Jacqueline had been her usual chatty self, but as she turned her attention from her friends to John, she sounded serious.

"Did you know that Betty and George broke up? Since he's going off to college in the fall and she's staying in Memphis for beauty school, they decided it was time to call it quits. Makes me sad, though. Have you decided what to do next year, John? I'm sure you've got offers to play football at several colleges, right? Everyone says you'll probably be following Frank to TSU."

John thought about how to answer, since the subject was still such a sensitive one at home. Of course he had struggled with his decision for months, but he dreaded the arguments he was going to get from Jacqueline and his other classmates, on top of the turmoil he was causing at home.

"Yes, I was approached by TSU and Jackson State and a couple more places, but I've decided not to play ball next year."

"What? But you were our star quarterback! And Frank is having a great time playing at TSU, isn't he? What are you thinking?"

"I'm thinking that I want to be a lawyer, Jacqueline. And first I want to get a top-notch liberal arts education at a university that will help me get into law school. It's the only way I can see to fight the racial injustices that don't seem to be getting any better."

Jacqueline looked shocked. "So, where are you going?"

"I'm going to Ole Miss."

"Ole Miss? If you're giving up football for a law career, why not go somewhere like Howard?"

"You know my parents can't afford to send me to Howard. And besides, going to a predominantly White university is an important part of the journey for me."

His words fell like lead and sat heavily in the silence between them. He had only told his parents a few weeks earlier, and the storm that followed at home hadn't calmed down completely yet. His father couldn't understand why he would waste his gridiron talent in order to follow in Meredith's footsteps and attend Ole Miss. Blacks wouldn't be allowed to play football at that school until 1973 when Robert "Gentle Ben" Williams would become the first African-American football player at the university.

"I want to study law," John had told his father.

"But you could get a full scholarship if you play ball at TSU or Jackson State," his father argued. "And be with your own people. At Ole Miss you're going to be in a minority, and no telling what all that will mean. If you think the little scuffles you've seen with White kids here in Memphis are bad, just wait 'til you're sitting next to them in university classrooms and eating with them in their cafeterias. And how fairly do you think those White professors are going to treat you? You think they care about your grades and getting you into their pearly-white law school?"

No telling, indeed. But John eventually won the argument and headed to Oxford, Mississippi as a freshman in the fall of 1966.

Adele was hanging on John's every word as he told his story. "That was fascinating, John. The sixties were certainly an apocalyptic time to grow up in the South. But I don't understand what all that has to do with Mary Margaret, or the book club, or Alzheimer's. What am I missing here?"

John glanced at Mary Margaret. “Oh, but it does. We’ll get to that soon enough.”

Mary Margaret cleared her throat as if readying herself to give a speech. “I think it’s my turn now. While John was growing up in Memphis, I was coming of age in a different hometown—in Jackson, Mississippi.”

“In Jackson?” Adele asked. “That’s where I’m from.”

“Yes, I remember you said that at book club the other night. And I think John would agree with me that the sixties in this tale of our two cities were ‘the best of times and the worst of times.’” Adele and John both laughed as Mary Margaret began her story.

What I do in writing of any character is to try to enter into the mind, heart, and skin of a human being who is not myself. Whether this happens to be a man or a woman, old or young, with skin black or white, the primary challenge lies in making the jump itself.

—**Eudora Welty,** *The Collected Stories*

CHAPTER 3

Mary Margaret (1960s)

Mary Margaret lived a charmed life with her upper-middle-class family in Jackson. Her father, David Sutherland, was a surgeon and her mother, Jeanne, was involved in every club available—Junior League, bridge, garden, and luncheon, and much to Mary Margaret's chagrin, the PTA at her high school. Jeanne had even convinced her busy doctor husband to join her and another parent couple in performing a song-and-dance routine in a musical fundraiser during Mary Margaret's sophomore year. That was the same year that Mary Margaret played Rebecca to her older brother's George in the school's production of *Our Town.* Maybe she did get the part because her brother Billy had the lead role, and she was a natural to play his younger sister on stage. But acting wasn't her main passion; she wanted to be a writer.

Her propensity started in junior high when she had a story published in her school's literary journal. By tenth grade she was already a feature writer for the high school newspaper, where she would end up as editor in her senior year. She even traveled to Chicago on a train to a national high school journalism conference that year. While many of her best friends were busy on the cheerleading squad or the drill team, Mary Margaret spent most of her free time reading. It's not that she wasn't pretty enough to be a cheerleader—she was one of the most beautiful girls in the school with her silky golden hair and sky blue eyes and perfect figure. But she loved books, especially Southern literature, and had been over-the-moon excited when she struck up a friendship in the summer of 1963 with one of Mississippi's most famous authors, her neighbor Eudora Welty.

Miss Welty's house was only a few blocks from the Sutherlands' in the historic Belhaven neighborhood, but Mary Margaret's first—and completely serendipitous—meeting with Miss Welty happened a few blocks away at their neighborhood Piggly Wiggly grocery store. Miss Welty was struggling with a bag of groceries as she dug around in her purse for her car keys when Mary Margaret approached her in the grocery store parking lot.

"May I help you?"

"Oh, yes, please. I should have gotten my keys out of my pocketbook before leaving the store. Can you hold this bag for me?"

Taking the sack of groceries from Miss Welty, Mary Margaret couldn't believe her luck. Of course, all the kids in the neighborhood knew the "popsicle lady" gave popsicles to kids who came by her house during the steamy hot summer months. But Mary Margaret always thought that was rude of the other kids, so she didn't join them. Once she began to read Miss Welty's short stories in junior high, she was hooked. And now to meet her in person was like Christmas in July!

"Would you like to come by my house for some sweet tea later?" Miss Welty asked as Mary Margaret placed the groceries in her car.

"Oh, my," she blushed, "I would love to. But I wouldn't want to interrupt your work."

Miss Welty laughed. "Oh goodness, honey, I never get any writing done in the afternoon. The early morning hours are best, while the subconscious is still alive with dreams and the brain is most open to creativity. In fact, you could just ride home with me now if you'd like, unless you need to be somewhere. You shopping for your mother?"

"Oh, no. I was actually just going to the Pig for a snack. Mom still does the grocery shopping for our family. I would love to join you."

"Do you live in Belhaven?"

"Oh, yes, ma'am. I'm Mary Margaret Sutherland. My family lives on Arlington."

Mary Margaret couldn't believe she was riding in the car with Eudora Welty, or following her inside her home, although it was only a few blocks from her own. And once inside the house, she was even more awestruck.

"Go on out on the porch and have a seat while I put these groceries away. I'll bring us some iced tea in a minute."

Should she follow Miss Welty to the kitchen and offer to help, or would that be too intrusive? Instead, she took a few minutes to peek into a room with a desk and typewriter, and stacks of books and paper everywhere—the inner sanctum of this world-famous writer. Maybe her talent would rub off on Mary Margaret!

Back out on the porch, she sat on a small loveseat sipping ice cold sweet tea served in a tall, thin crystal glass. As Miss Welty took her seat on a nearby chair, Mary Margaret's mind flooded with questions. Before she could begin, Miss Welty picked up a copy of *The New Yorker* off a nearby wicker table and handed it to her. "Have you seen this yet?" It was dated July 6, 1963. Just a week earlier.

Mary Margaret took the magazine. "No ma'am. In fact, I don't believe I've ever seen this magazine at all. What's it about?"

"How old are you, child?"

"I'm fourteen. Just finished ninth grade."

"Well, I don't imagine you have read *The New Yorker* yet. Have you seen it around your house? Perhaps your parents read it?"

Mary Margaret shook her head, looking somewhat embarrassed for herself and her parents. "Should they have?"

Miss Welty laughed. "Well, I guess that depends a bit on their political leanings. Did they vote for Nixon or Kennedy?"

"Um, Nixon, I believe. I don't really pay that much attention to politics. I'm more into literature, mainly fiction . . . I want to be a writer . . . like you. I am a great admirer of your work, ma'am."

Miss Welty smiled gently. "Well, young lady, it's time you learn that you can't learn about the world around you just by reading short stories and novels. Or by writing them. Where do you think writers get their ideas from?"

Mary Margaret shrugged and sipped more of her tea, wishing that she could be the one asking the questions. Trying to sound more mature, she asked, "Why did you show me this magazine? Do you have a short story published in it or something?"

"Good question, and indeed, I do."

"Oh, good, I was hoping so." Mary Margaret was eager to discuss literature. She loved some of Eudora Welty's early stories like "Why I Live at the P. O."

"Well," Miss Welty said as she poured more tea, "my story in this magazine is called, 'Where Is the Voice Coming From?' and I wrote it because of what happened to Medgar Evers last month. You do know who Medgar Evers is, don't you?"

"Oh, yes, ma'am. We saw that on the news. Terrible that he was shot."

"Yes, it was. And I wrote a story about it the very night of the shooting. It's fiction, and it's from the point of view of the killer."

"So, you think what the killer did was right?" Mary Margaret asked, confused.

"Oh, no, dear. Not at all. But I wanted to understand why he did it. What was he thinking? What moved him to do such an awful deed? If you want to be a writer—or at any rate a good one—you've got to get into your characters' heads, whether they are good or bad."

Mary Margaret nodded. "Um, could I borrow this so I can read the story?"

Miss Welty smiled. "Of course. I've got more copies. Maybe your parents will even read it. Come back and visit another day and tell me what you think of it."

"Yes, ma'am." Mary Margaret held the magazine close to her heart, like it was a treasure. She wanted to sound intelligent, to show Miss Welty that she wasn't some dumb kid. But maybe she was. There was so much going on in the world—and especially in her hometown—that she didn't understand.

As if reading Mary Margaret's thoughts, Miss Welty asked, "What are your friends saying about all of this racial unrest?"

Mary Margaret shrugged. "Not much, why?"

"Did y'all discuss it before school let out in June? What did your teachers say? Did they talk about events that happened right here in Jackson, like the sit-in at Woolworth's the last week of May?"

"I . . . I think I heard about it, but no, we didn't really discuss it at school. I guess we were busy with exams and getting excited about school being out for the summer. Can you remind me what happened?"

Miss Welty took a deep breath and another sip of tea as she gathered her thoughts. "I think it was May 28. Some students from Tougaloo College—one White girl and two Negroes—went to Woolworth's with one of their teachers, a White man, and they sat down together at the 'Whites Only' lunch counter."

"Did they order lunch?"

"No, they didn't get a chance because no one would take their orders. No one would serve them."

"Because they were at the 'Whites Only' counter?"

"That's right. And that's what they were protesting. They sat there a long time, and lots of people came into the store and gathered around them, including a number of policemen. And not just adults—there were White students from Central High School who came in on their lunch break. Some of them started calling the Negro students and the professor names, and then they picked up the ketchup and mustard and sugar from the counter and started pouring it all over them."

"That's awful. Didn't the police do anything to stop them?"

"No. Not even when someone pulled one of the students off a counter stool and started kicking him in the face. They just watched. Finally the police stopped him, and yes, they arrested the person doing the kicking, but they also arrested the student who was being kicked."

"What for?"

"I guess for sitting at the 'Whites Only' lunch counter."

Mary Margaret's head was spinning from feeling something she hadn't felt before, maybe a mixture of anger over the injustice, but also sadness. Not just sadness for Blacks, but for the world as she had known it up until now, her fifteenth year.

"What happened next?"

"More violence. Someone even punched the White Tougaloo professor in the face. After several hours the store manager told them to leave, but they couldn't get out through the crowd. The police wouldn't even help them. Finally, the president of Tougaloo College—who had been called—arrived and helped them through the mob, but people threw things at them as they made their way to his car."

"I—I can't believe all this happened and none of my teachers even mentioned it, or my parents."

"Most White people don't want to get involved. Don't want their world to change. Or they're just scared. But this is probably just the beginning of lots of protests . . . lots of violence. You'll be in the thick of it in the coming years, and you'll have to decide how you're going to respond to it. Especially when you get to college."

"Yes, ma'am. It's sure a lot to think about."

Miss Welty stood and carried her glass to the kitchen counter. She turned and looked at Mary Margaret. "I've got to get supper started now. I have a guest coming in a couple of hours. Do you need a ride home?"

"Oh, no thank you. We just live a few blocks from here. I can walk. Thank you so much for the tea and the visit."

Mary Margaret took her time walking home. She was eager to tell her mother about her visit with Eudora Welty and show her the magazine, but she was anxious about discussing racial issues with her. Distracted by her thoughts as she walked through the back door into the kitchen, she almost ran into her brother Billy, who was on his way out.

"Hey! Watch where you're going!" Billy teased.

"Oh, sorry. Where are you off to?"

"Out." It was the summer after Billy's junior year in high school. He had gotten his own car, and with it came a newfound freedom.

"Out with Jenny?" She loved to tease him about his girlfriend.

"None of your beeswax, kid!" He smiled as he turned to leave, shouting over his shoulder, "Bye, Mom. I won't be home for supper."

Jeanne Sutherland was in the kitchen cooking her husband's favorite meal—lasagna. The house smelled like sausage and oregano and basil. Mary Margaret stepped over to the stove to taste the sauce as her mother was preparing to pour it over the layers of pasta and ricotta cheese. Her mother chided her gently. "Careful, that's hot. You'll burn your mouth. And by the way, where have you been? I thought you were just walking to the Piggly Wiggly for a snack."

"You'll never believe it, Mom. I ran into Eudora Welty in the parking lot at the Pig. She needed help getting her groceries into her car, and she ended up inviting me to her house. We've been having iced tea and talking about writing . . . and other stuff. Can you imagine that?"

"Oh, that was nice, but I hope you didn't bother her. Would you turn the oven on? Three-fifty, please?"

"Yes ma'am. So, she loaned me a copy of *The New Yorker* magazine." Mary Margaret fetched the magazine from a nearby chair and put it on the kitchen counter so her mother could see it.

"Uh, huh. And why did she give you that magazine?"

"Because it has a short story she wrote in it! Isn't that cool? She asked if you and Dad ever read *The New Yorker*, and I told her I didn't know. Do y'all read it, Mom?"

"Not really, dear." She moved about the kitchen gracefully assembling the lasagna and washing the pasta pot in the sink as they talked. "Your father doesn't really have time to read much of anything but his medical journals. And I prefer inspirational books like Taylor Caldwell's *Dear and Glorious Physician*—you know, the one about the Apostle Luke?"

"Aren't you even curious about Miss Welty's story?"

"Oh, Mary Margaret, you know I'm not into serious literature. Why don't you read it and tell me all about it? Now will you please hold the oven door open for me? This lasagna is heavy."

"Sure." Mary Margaret never stopped talking as she opened the oven door and then closed it after her mother put the lasagna in. "But about Miss Welty's story. What I know so far is she wrote it the night Medgar Evers was assassinated."

"Assassinated is kind of a strong word, don't you think?"

"Well, what would you call it, mother?"

Her mother took off her apron and hung it on a hook and looked at Mary Margaret. "I would call it not something a young lady your age needs to worry about. This is your summer vacation and you'll be a sophomore in the fall. You should be thinking about all the fun things girls your age are doing. Like getting a tan at the country club pool and learning to play bridge and going to summer camp."

"Well, what about the sit-in at the Woolworth's counter last month? Is that something a young lady my age should know about, or not? You know there were Negro students from Central High School involved. They're my age."

"Oh, I'm sure that will blow over soon, if it hasn't already. Now go and wash up for dinner, please."

The conversation with her father later that night didn't go much differently. Both her parents seemed to be living in some sort of protective bubble where things like racial injustice and civil rights just weren't part of their world. And in reality, Mary Margaret's world was also isolated from what was going on in her city, and throughout the South. Her segregated high school wouldn't have Blacks until the year after she graduated, so her only interaction with people of color was with her family's maid, Lillie Bell. But Eudora Welty had pried open the teenager's eyes to a whole new part of the world.

The next week, Mary Margaret read Eudora Welty's short story in *The New Yorker* and a few editorials in the *Jackson Clarion Ledger* newspaper about the Evers shooting, making her eager for another visit with Miss Welty. She didn't have Miss Welty's phone number, so she decided to drop by her house one afternoon around four, remembering that she had said she did her writing in the mornings. She clutched *The New Yorker* in one hand and rang the doorbell with the other. As she waited, she looked across the street at the stately buildings of Belhaven College and wondered what it would be like to be a college student one day. Would she be on the newspaper staff? Would she learn to write amazing stories like Eudora Welty? And for the first time, she also wondered if there would be any Black students at her college.

As if listening to her thoughts, Miss Welty—who had been standing with the door open —startled Mary Margaret saying, "Do you want to come in, or would you rather just stand there daydreaming?"

Mary Margaret jumped and then laughed. "Oh, I'm so sorry, Miss Welty. And yes, I was daydreaming about going to college, actually. And maybe becoming a writer like you one day."

Miss Welty laughed. "Don't get ahead of yourself. It's time to enjoy what's left of your childhood first. And didn't you say you'd be a sophomore in high school this fall?"

"Yes, ma'am," Mary Margaret replied, as she followed Miss Welty inside. This time they stopped in the kitchen, where Miss Welty motioned for Mary Margaret to sit at the table.

"I'm having another cup of coffee. Can I offer you something? Maybe a Coke?"

"That would be great." Mary Margaret set the copy of *The New Yorker* on the table as she relaxed in the chair, taking in the surroundings again.

"I see you brought back the magazine," Miss Welty said, as she poured her coffee, opened the bottle of Coke, and joined Mary Margaret at the table. "I said you could keep it. Let me guess—your parents didn't want it in the house?"

Mary Margaret looked puzzled.

"They don't read *The New Yorker*, do they?"

"No, I guess not. Mother said Dad doesn't have time. He only reads medical journals and the Sunday paper, and she mainly reads Christian inspirational books, if she reads at all. I couldn't even get them to read your story about the assassination. Mother said I was too young to be worrying about such things."

Miss Welty nodded and grinned. "That's not surprising. She was raised a certain way, and she sees you as an extension of the culture she came up in. We all do that. It takes a strong disposition and a lot of courage to do anything that disturbs the status quo."

"Is that what you do with your writing?"

"Sometimes. Not always on purpose. But writing that story about Evers' assassination was disturbing because I wanted it to be. What did you think about it?"

Mary Margaret sipped her Coke and picked up the magazine, holding it in her hands as though touching Miss Welty's words would somehow bestow her wisdom. "I'm not sure. It kind of scared me, you know? To think that someone could be so angry with another person just because their skin was a different color. Angry enough to kill them. Did you know much about the man who killed Mr. Evers? Beckwith, I think his name was?"

"Not personally, but I didn't need to know him. I grew up in a culture of hatred toward Negroes. The assassin I wrote about could have been any one of hundreds of ignorant White men."

Mary Margaret stared straight into Miss Welty's face as she spoke, mesmerized by the way she talked, and imagining her own future life as a writer. "Are all of your stories like this one?" she asked.

"No, they're all different. But in each one I try to get into the mind of the people I write about, even though they are fictional. That's the hard part about writing, but also what makes it so worthwhile."

"Yes, ma'am, I can understand that. I'm hoping to be on the newspaper staff in high school this fall. Would you mind if I show you some of my stories some day?"

"I would love that, Mary Margaret. But what about the rest of your summer? Will you be doing any writing while you're out of school?"

"I won't really have time since I'll be going to Camp Desoto for a month soon. But I'd love to stay in touch and maybe we can visit again one day."

Mary Margaret was surprised by Miss Welty's hug as she stood up to leave. She could feel a kindred spirit in that embrace, and the feeling stayed with her on her walk home.

The Sutherlands' maid, Lillie Bell, was cleaning Mary Margaret's bedroom when she got there.

"Hi, Miss Mary Margaret!" She was always cheerful. And she always treated Mary Margaret and her brother like they were special. But she wondered why Lillie Bell called her "Miss" instead of by her first name—she was only fourteen. She also was unsure why she addressed Lillie Bell by her first name and not "Mrs." Mary Margaret realized, *I don't even know her last name.* She decided to ask Lillie Bell about it.

"Hi, Lillie Bell. I was just wondering about something."

"Well, spit it out."

"I was wondering why you call me 'Miss' Mary Margaret, but I just call you by your first name. You're older than my mother, but I call her friends 'Mrs.'"

"Oh, child," Lillie Bell, said as she continued dusting Mary Margaret's bookshelves. "It's just the way it's always been done."

"But that doesn't make it right, does it?"

Lillie Bell just looked at Mary Margaret and shrugged.

"So," Mary Margaret continued, "what is your last name, anyway?"

"Well, I was born a Hebert, but when I married Gus, I took his name, so it's Williams."

"You're married? How come I never knew that? I thought you lived by yourself."

"I do. Gus couldn't get work here, so he went up to Chicago 'bout ten years ago. Was sending me checks regular like until he got killed."

Mary Margaret nearly fell onto the bed that Lillie Bell was trying to make up.

"Child, if you're not going to help me, at least don't keep me from doing my work," she said with a smile.

"I just can't believe I didn't know any of this."

"Oh, honey, you were just a child."

Lillie Bell stopped cleaning the room and sat on the bed next to Mary Margaret. She pulled her into a hug, which reminded Mary Margaret of how she used to sit in her lap when she was a little girl. Lillie Bell would sing to her and soothe her when she was upset. She now wanted to know more about this woman who had taken such good care of her all these years.

After a few minutes, Lillie Bell got up to leave the room. Just as she reached the door, Mary Margaret called out, "Thank you. Thank you for cleaning my room, Mrs. Williams."

Lillie Bell smiled and shook her head, and headed on to her duties in the rest of the house.

Those visits with Eudora Welty in the summer of 1963 would turn out to be life-changing for Mary Margaret. As she moved through her sophomore and junior years of high school, she continued to read everything she could find that Miss Welty had written, along with the required classics and a long list of other Southern writers—most especially William Faulkner. And she achieved her dream of writing for the school newspaper her junior year, starting with a piece about the Civil Rights Act of 1964. Proudly showing the article to her mother after school the day the paper came out, she didn't get the response she was hoping for.

"Oh, honey. Why are you involving yourself in all those upsetting issues? Why don't you write about something that makes people happy?"

"Like what, Mom? You want me to write about fashion and bridge clubs? Don't you think it's important for people my age to be informed about what's going on in the world outside of the country club?" She didn't wait for an answer, but stormed out of the kitchen into her room to read her article in print. Her heart pounded as she read the title of her article in large print: *How Does the Civil Rights Act Affect Students?* And when she saw her name in the byline she almost swooned. Her article pointed out that most of the congressmen from Southern states like Mississippi voted against the Act. She challenged her fellow students to consider the changes that this bill would have on their way of life. Would they welcome those changes? How would they feel about their school being integrated some day? And other public places? What about Negroes being allowed to have jobs that only Whites currently have, and to receive equal pay?

But the *rights* guaranteed by this historic law didn't touch her life during her final two years of high school, as she continued to live in the bubble her parents created and inhabited—the one they expected her to stay within. Even cataclysmic events like the signing of the Voting Rights Law, Martin Luther King, Jr.'s march in Alabama, and the riots in Watts—all during her junior year and the following summer of 1965—felt like they were miles away from her homogenous high school and neighborhood. And that's exactly how her parents liked it— especially her mother. She was only interested in Mary Margaret's elite social life.

Jeanne was always pushing Mary Margaret to flirt with the boys, or at least to pay attention when they flirted with her. Of course the boys were interested in Mary Margaret, but she disappointed most of them by keeping her nose in books and newspapers most of the time. Or by leaving town for camp, as she did for the last time in the summer before her senior year.

"Mary Margaret!" her mother called from the kitchen. "Telephone!"

As she came into the kitchen, Mary Margaret noticed her mother was smiling broadly. With her hand covering the receiver, she whispered, "I think it's Adam Wentworth."

Adam was already a star on the basketball team, and his family came from what her mother called "old money."

Mary Margaret grabbed the receiver and stretched its long curly cord out into the hallway, shutting the kitchen door behind her. "Hello," she spoke matter-of-factly.

"Hi, Margaret. This is Adam. I was hoping to catch you before you leave for camp again. You headed back to Desoto this summer?"

"Yep. It's my last year as a camper."

"So, I was wondering if you'd like to do something before you leave."

"Do something like what?"

"Well, how about going sailing with me out at the reservoir tomorrow? Dad said I could use the dinghy."

Sailing sounded like fun, so Mary Margaret accepted Adam's invitation and found herself enjoying the sun and water and breeze the next day. Adam was a looker, and he could sing. Late in the afternoon as they pulled back into the marina, he sang the Righteous Brothers' new hit, "Unchained Melody," and she felt something strange stir in her. As they sat at the end of the dock watching the brilliant orange sunset over the water, she even let him kiss her. No promises were made, but she did wonder if he would call her again when school started back.

As her senior year rolled around, Mary Margaret became editor of the school paper and secretary of the Student Council. Adam led their basketball team to a state championship and tried to lead Mary

Margaret into the backseat of his car more than once. Even though she attended all his games, she tried to keep their relationship casual. She made lots of attempts to engage him in serious discussions about the things that mattered to her—especially the Vietnam War, which the United States had just entered in March of 1965. Another topic she pressed was the shooting of James Meredith during their senior year, just as he was marching through Mississippi.

"Do you even know who James Meredith is?" Mary Margaret asked Adam during one of their talks at the soda fountain at Brent's Drugs after school.

"Of course I know who he is, Mary Margaret," Adam scoffed. "He's that Negro who caused such a fuss enrolling at Ole Miss a few years ago. But I just don't know what you think that has to do with us, or why you're always talking about what's happening with the Negroes, instead of just having a good time. And please don't tell me that he has anything to do with you going to Ole Miss next year."

"Well, I do think it took a lot of courage for him to go to school there, but you know I'm going because that's where my parents went. And there aren't many Negro students at Ole Miss yet, so my mother doesn't have to worry about me having too many 'colored' friends."

As Mary Margaret sailed through her senior year with perfect grades and lots of honors, her mother obsessed over her daughter's plans for the next year—specifically, which sorority she would pledge at Ole Miss. It was a given that she would go to her parents' alma mater, and since her mother was a Tri Delta legacy, that also seemed to be a tradition she was expected to follow.

Adam headed off to Mississippi State on a basketball scholarship, leaving Mary Margaret to enter the ranks of the smart, beautiful, and available freshman girls flooding the Ole Miss campus in the fall of 1966.

My continuing passion is to part a curtain, that invisible veil of indifference that falls between us and that blinds us to each other's presence, each other's wonder, each other's human plight.

—Eudora Welty

CHAPTER 4

Ole Miss (1966)

As expected, Mary Margaret pledged Tri Delt (Delta Delta Delta) sorority and was even elected president of her pledge class, which kept her pretty busy—not that she needed something to occupy her time. She joined the staff of the student newspaper, *The Daily Mississippian,* which published five days a week, but lost interest after her sophomore year as her love for literature increased. Even with her major in education—never considering a different path than teaching—she always carved out time to read for pleasure, preserving her dream of being a writer.

Mary Margaret's metaphorical dance card was always full, as she was sought after by many of the campus's most eligible men. She enjoyed the fraternity parties and balls, and especially the weekend picnics and sailing at Sardis Lake with friends and their dates. She wasn't in a hurry for a serious relationship, and frankly, none of the boys—yes, she considered them boys—impressed her enough to sustain more than one or two dates. That would soon change.

John was one of only a few dozen Black students at the university his freshman year, and at first he kept to himself most of the time, majoring in pre-law and spending many hours at the library. He didn't have many friends on campus, so he went home to Memphis most weekends, proving his father's point that he would be "without his people" in Oxford. Back home, there were always local girls hoping for a date, and weekends watching his brother play football for TSU. But each time he returned to school, he remembered why he was there, and he gradually began to stay on campus more. That's when he began to notice Mary Margaret in their freshman English class. He was struck by her beauty, but also her love for literature. And she couldn't help but admire his answers to questions in class. She was a bit embarrassed to find herself surprised that a Negro would sound so intelligent. John even scored higher than she did on their last exam. One day after class, she made the first move.

"Would you like to study together for the Faulkner exam?" Her blue eyes twinkled and her blond ponytail shone in the sunshine as they walked outside after class one day.

Surprised by her invitation, John felt awkward with his reply. "I guess so." He looked around at the other students—all White—who were walking near them as they left the building. "We could grab some lunch at the union and study there, or over at the Grove since it's so pretty outside today." John's heart fluttered as he anticipated spending time with Mary Margaret outside class.

"Well," Mary Margaret paused, choosing her next words carefully, "I eat at the house—The Tri Delt house—but I could meet you at the Grove around one-thirty. Or you could come over to the house, and we could study there after lunch."

"Are you sure that would be okay? For me to be at your sorority house, I mean?" John looked at the ground and shuffled his feet nervously. Somehow, the thought of a young Black man inside a sorority house on the Ole Miss campus conjured up images of white-jacketed waiters at a country club. "Are Blacks even allowed in there?"

"I—I haven't ever thought about it," Mary Margaret said.

"Well, have you ever seen any Black students at your sorority house?" John pressed.

"No, I guess not. But it's high time that changed. Boys aren't allowed for meals, but why don't you come on over around one-fifteen and we'll study in the living room. It's quiet there."

"Okay. See you then."

At lunch at the student union, John saw a couple of his friends eating with several other Black students. There were fewer than 200 African Americans enrolled at the university, which had about 7,000 students altogether. Eddie waved him over. "Hey, John, come join us."

John slid into a seat next to Eddie and across from Dianna. They knew each other from participating in Black student activities on campus. Otherwise, they really didn't hang out together, as John stayed busy with his studies.

"We missed you at the meeting last week," Eddie said. "Where you been?"

"Oh, sorry. Guess I forgot. I'm also buried in work this semester."

"Oh, yeah, man, you're pre-law, right?"

John nodded. "What did y'all talk about at the meeting?"

"Not much new. Same old issues that don't seem to be getting any attention from the administration. Brothers finding threatening notes under their dorm doors and even loud knocks in the middle of the night."

"What do y'all do when those White boys block the sidewalk and won't let you by?" Dianna asked.

"I aint' gonna fight with 'em, so I just walk around them—ruined a good pair of shoes in the mud the other day," Eddie said.

"And not much support from any Whites, really," John said.

"No surprise there," Dianna said. "My mother worked as a maid at one of the women's residence halls for years, and later at one of the sorority houses, and she said she never heard those White girls talking seriously about civil rights. They're just too caught up in their own little worlds—more concerned about marrying rich guys and moving up the social ladder."

John nodded and dove into his hamburger and fries.

Dianna looked at Eddie, then back at John. "Didn't I see you walking with Mary Margaret Sutherland over near Ventress a few minutes ago?"

"Uh, yeah. We have English together. How do you know her name?"

"She's on the *Mississippian* staff. I've seen her picture there. But hey, don't change the subject. It looks like you two have more than an interest in books."

"What? She asked me to study with her for an exam."

"Uh huh." Dianna and Eddie said in unison.

"Hey, I've got a class. See y'all later." Dianna got up and left.

Eddie put his arm on John's shoulder. "Just be careful with that girl, okay? I know we're hoping things will be different soon, but I'm not sure how her White friends are going to feel about y'all hanging out together." He patted John on the back as he got up to leave.

John sat staring at his lunch and realized he had lost his appetite. Should he listen to Eddie's warning? He was nervous as a cat as he walked down Sorority Row and stopped at the door to the Delta Delta Delta house, with its historic red brick walls and stately white columns. Should he knock? Just as he was trying to decide what to do, a pretty, young coed came up the steps behind him and said, "Deliveries are around back."

"Oh, no, I'm not delivering anything. I'm here to see Mary Margaret . . . I mean, Miss Sutherland. We're going to study together."

The girl stared at him in disbelief. After a moment of silence, she replied, "Oh, I see. Well, I guess you can come in then."

John followed her into the foyer. Girls were coming and going from the nearby dining room where lunch was just finishing up, and ascending and descending the staircase that led to their sleeping quarters upstairs. An attractive middle-aged woman dressed in a polyester knit suit approached John. "May I help you?"

"Yes, ma'am. I'm John Abbott. I'm here to study with Mary Margaret Sutherland. We have English class together." He looked around nervously, wishing he and Mary Margaret had made plans to study at the Grove or the library, anywhere but here! Just then, Mary Margaret came into the foyer.

"Oh, there you are, John. I see you've met Mrs. Murray, our house mother."

"We haven't formally met, but John was just telling me he's here to study with you. Is that true?" Mrs. Murray's eyes never left John's, even as she addressed Mary Margaret.

"Yes, ma'am. We've got an English exam coming up." Mary Margaret smiled nonchalantly at John and Mrs. Murray, swinging her ponytail confidently as she moved towards the stairs. "John knows more about Faulkner than I do, that's for sure!"

John hung his head, embarrassed by her compliment.

"I'll be right back down. I've got to run upstairs and get my notes. Mrs. Murray, will you please show John into the living room?"

When Mary Margaret got to her room upstairs her roommate was waiting.

"Oh, hi, Shannon. I didn't see you at lunch. You feeling okay?"

"I'm fine. I was working on an art project and lost track of the time. I'll grab a sandwich later."

Mary Margaret retied the bow on her ponytail and put on lipstick before grabbing her Faulkner notes. "Well, I'm going to study for an exam in the living room. See you later."

"Wait a minute, Mary Margaret." Shannon stopped her. "I think I ran into your study partner when I was coming in the front door a few minutes ago."

"Oh, you met John? He's so nice. And super smart. He's pre-law."

"I'm sure he's nice, but aren't you concerned at all about, well, about what people are going to think?"

"Think about what, Shannon?" Mary Margaret was getting irritated, knowing Shannon grew up on a former plantation in the Mississippi Delta.

"You know what I mean. Just be careful."

Mrs. Murray was quiet as she led John into the well-appointed living area, where several other girls were already ensconced in the over-stuffed chairs and sofas, textbooks and pens and papers spread out around them. "Y'all can work over there." She pointed to a small square table with four chairs around it.

"Thank you." John settled into one of the chairs and opened his notebook to the pages where he had written a few potential discussion questions on Faulkner's *The Sound and the Fury.* Several pairs of eyes watched as he tried to concentrate on the words in front of him. Finally, Mary Margaret joined him at the table.

"Ready to get started?" Her question—even the tone in her voice—showed none of the discomfort that John was feeling.

"I guess so. Your house mother didn't seem too happy to see me, though."

"Oh, she'll get over it. There's a first time for everything. Like Dylan said, 'the times they are a-changin.'"

John and Mary Margaret studied together that afternoon and several more times in the coming days. On pretty afternoons they sat on a blanket in the Grove, enjoying the crisp fall air and the show of colors put on by the trees. The red and sugar maples were the prettiest of the dozens of species in the fall. Lots of other students were studying there, or tossing Frisbees or just taking walks. But the beauty of their surroundings did little to erase the judgmental stares the couple received every time they were together in public. It wasn't any different in the library, where the silence only accentuated the palpable racial tension. And yet their love for Southern literature seemed to morph seamlessly into a growing mutual attraction. Finally, John got up the courage to ask her for a date to an upcoming football game.

Mary Margaret didn't hesitate with her answer. "I'd love to. Drop by the house around seven and we'll walk to the stadium together."

Saturday night arrived, and John waited anxiously for Mary Margaret in the foyer at the house. When she came downstairs, amidst the flutter of a houseful of her sorority sisters heading out the door with their dates, she greeted him with her characteristic dimpled smile. Her long hair—loose from its usual ponytail—was swept gracefully across her navy cardigan. Her white blouse with its Peter Pan collar was tucked into a navy and red plaid skirt.

"You look great," John said as she came down the stairs. He was dressed in khaki pants and a navy blazer, with a baby blue shirt and red and blue plaid tie. "Guess we're sporting our red and blue for the game, huh?" He held the front door open and they walked down the brick steps towards the street.

But once they were outside on the sidewalk headed towards the stadium, someone yelled at John from the street, "Hey, nigger! What do you think you're doing?"

Mary Margaret and John stopped walking and looked around at Mary Margaret's friends and their dates, who were also stopped in their tracks by the outburst.

"Just ignore him. He's an idiot," Mary Margaret said, grabbing hold of John's hand. The other couples filing out of the Tri Delt house stared and whispered to one another as they continued walking to the game.

The crowd thickened as the couple entered the stadium and found their seats, amidst quite a few stares, but there were no verbal or physical attacks. As the excitement of the ballgame heated up, everyone seemed to forget about the biracial couple bucking the social mores of this Southern school.

Coach Johnny Vaught and his star quarterback, Bruce Newell, dominated the crowd's conversations. Ole Miss beat Southern Mississippi 14-7 that night, and the campus was bursting with school spirit as students poured out of the stadium and into the fraternity houses for the after-game parties. As John and Mary Margaret walked back towards the Tri Delt house, he asked if she'd like to go somewhere to celebrate. Since there were no Black fraternities on campus, they were a couple without a country on this typical game night at Ole Miss.

Mary Margaret felt the loneliness of their predicament, as her sorority sisters were all headed to parties with their dates. John had an old 1959 Chevrolet Bel Air parked in the lot by his dorm, so they walked over to his car, climbed into the front seat, and sat looking at each other expectantly.

"I guess we should have talked about what to do after the game," John offered.

"It's not like I didn't think about it," Mary Margaret said. "But I didn't want to bring it up to make you feel bad or anything."

After a minute of awkward silence, John said, "Do you like the blues?"

"Music? Oh, I guess that sounded stupid. I'm not sure. I mean, most of the music we have at parties on campus is either rock 'n roll or Motown. Why?"

"Well, there's a band called The Checkmates that plays at a club out on Old Sardis Road. Are you up for a different kind of cultural experience? You'll probably be the only White person there."

Mary Margaret held her hand across her abdomen to calm a growing knot. "I guess so. But we have to be back by midnight for curfew at the house."

"Of course."

Forty-five minutes later, they pulled up into the gravel parking lot at Tom Charlie's, and John got the door for Mary Margaret. As they entered the smoke-filled club, lead singer Henry Cook was just getting warmed up on stage, and the all-Black audience was mingling at the bar and the small tables scattered between the bar and the stage. It was Mary Margaret's turn to be the focus of the stares now, as all eyes were trained on her. John led her to a corner table on the far side of the bar and settled her into a chair before asking what she'd like to drink.

"I'll have a Coke."

"You sure that's all you want? They don't check IDs here."

"Yeah, I'm sure."

John left her at the table and went to the bar to get their drinks. Mary Margaret played with a stray curl that had escaped her barrette and looked nervously around the club. Most of the couples that stared as she and John walked in had gone back to watching the stage from their tables or moving rhythmically on the dance floor. John returned with their drinks and smiled as he watched Mary Margaret take in the scene.

"You're not in Kansas anymore," he grinned.

She laughed. "Okay, I've never heard music like this before. I like it, but I admit that it feels weird in here. How do you ever get used to being in the minority so much of your life?"

"I don't get used to it. I'd like to be part of changing the culture, but there's a lot of history behind the way things are, especially in the South."

"You ever thought of moving away?"

"Not really. I'd rather stay and try to make things better. That's why I want to go to law school and work as a civil rights lawyer in Memphis one day. Or maybe even become a judge."

"Wow. You dream big."

"Why do you say that? You mean because I'm Black?"

"Okay, I can see how that sounded disrespectful. But what I meant was, that's a big goal for any college student, not just because of your race."

"What about your goals? With your love for Southern writers, are you going to become a writer yourself?"

Mary Margaret laughed. "That was my dream when I was younger, but Mother said I should be practical and major in Education so I can get a job teaching school. Hopefully, I'll get married and have kids." She blushed and looked away as she said that. "Of course, my folks want me to settle in Jackson, where I grew up."

"That all sounds so idyllic, and safe."

Mary Margaret let John's words settle in her mind as she sipped her Coke and listened to the blues floating through the room and into her heart. Several of the couples were slow dancing, their bodies moving as one to the sultry sounds coming from the band. John noticed her watching.

"Want to dance?"

That knot in her stomach returned, but she nodded and he took her hand and led her onto the dance floor. Henry Cook was singing "When A Man Loves a Woman," and several couples were making out on the dance floor. John held her close and she closed her eyes, trying to think only of the two of them and not of this unfamiliar place and people. John leaned down to whisper something in her ear, and as his cheek brushed hers, she felt a new sensation. Of course she had slow danced with other boys. Even been kissed by a few. Why did this feel so different? She wanted to believe it had nothing to do with race, though she had never been this close to a Black boy before.

She found herself wishing he would move his hand lower on her back, pull her closer. She wanted to move in the same sensual way she noticed the other couples in the room doing. His body seemed to sense her longing, and just when he was beginning to pull her closer and they were getting lost in the music, an alarm sounded in her head.

She pulled away from him suddenly and looked at her watch. "It's eleven o'clock. We've got to go or I'll miss curfew!" John reluctantly escorted her out the door just as the song ended.

Several couples were hanging out in the parking lot, smoking and talking. John smiled and nodded as they walked by. Mary Margaret felt guilty that their presence made her nervous. Once they were safely in John's car, she moved closer to him on the front seat.

"I'm really glad you brought me here, John."

Their eyes found each other's through the dim lights from the club, and John leaned down towards her face. The kiss was unlike anything either of them had experienced—tender but also very primal. She wanted more, but she didn't want to miss curfew at the house, so she moved reluctantly back across the seat and John started the engine.

They were both quiet on the ride back to campus, and when they pulled up in front of the Tri Delt house there were groups of kids everywhere. As John opened the car door for Mary Margaret, several couples approached. Before Mary Margaret could even speak to her sorority sisters who were returning from their parties, one of their dates yelled at John, "What do you think you're doing, boy?" Before John could answer, the White guy charged and punched him in the face. When John started to get up, another boy kicked him back down on the sidewalk.

Mary Margaret jumped from the car and screamed as she knelt to help John, who was conscious but bleeding from the nose and mouth. She looked at the boy who had hit him, a junior basketball player named Jimbo, and his date—her friend Carol Ann—who did nothing to come to her aid.

Mary Margaret yelled up at Jimbo from the sidewalk. "Are you crazy? He wasn't doing anything wrong, you hateful bigot!" She looked pleadingly at Carol Ann, who seemed to be frozen in place.

By then a crowd had gathered and a couple of other boys pulled Jimbo and his friend away from the sidewalk, and the couples all began moving towards the front door of the house.

"Are you okay?" Mary Margaret asked as she helped John to his feet. "Do you want me to call the campus police?"

"No, I'm fine. But I think you might want to head on inside by yourself. I don't want to cause you any more embarrassment."

"*Embarrassment?* You were just assaulted, John. Jimbo and that other idiot are the ones who should be embarrassed. Or arrested!"

"And how do you think that would play out, with nothing but a bunch of White kids as witnesses to what happened? You think they're going to stick up for me? Let's just leave it alone, Mary Margaret."

Mary Margaret wanted to keep arguing with him. To tell him to walk her to the door like the other boys were doing with their dates.

But she knew he wouldn't listen. Tears flowed as she watched John walk around to the other side of his car and drive away.

When she walked up the steps to the front door of the sorority house, Mrs. Murray was waiting for her. "You're late, young lady."

"Yes ma'am. I'm sorry, but those boys assaulted John and I was trying to help him." Mrs. Murray put her arm around her shoulder and escorted her inside the house.

"Come back to my apartment, and let's talk about this."

Mary Margaret sat on one of the flowered chintz chairs in Mrs. Murray's parlor and Mrs. Murray brought her a cup of tea from her kitchenette. A portrait of her family on the wall reminded Mary Margaret of the life Mrs. Murray lived before her husband died and she moved into the Tri Delt house for her position as house mother. Pictures of her grandchildren in small silver frames sat on lace doilies on the pecan coffee table.

"Now, let's talk about what happened tonight," Mrs. Murray began.

"It started when we left for the game. Some frat boys started calling John names." Mary Margaret's hands were shaking as she picked up the teacup, so she set it back down on the saucer and held her hands together in her lap. "Everything was okay at the game." She purposely didn't tell Mrs. Murray about going to the blues club. "Nothing really happened until we came back at the end of the evening. That's when those boys attacked John."

Mrs. Murray was quiet as she sipped her tea, handing Mary Margaret a tissue. When she spoke, her voice was firm but compassionate.

"What did you think was going to happen, dear? I'm sure John is a fine boy, but his presence on campus—along with the other Negroes—is something that's going to take people a while to get used to. If you date him, I'm afraid you're just asking for trouble."

They both sat quietly for a minute before Mrs. Murray continued.

"Mary Margaret, I'm curious about your interest in John, and your willingness to be ostracized for being involved with him. I wouldn't have expected you to be so, well, so radical. You grew up in a privileged home and society. What is it that draws you into John's world?"

Mary Margaret's hands had quit shaking, so she finished her tea while considering her response.

"Several things, actually. For one, we have a Negro maid, Lillie Bell, who has worked for our family since I was a baby. I love her dearly, and I know my parents appreciate her, but I don't think they respect her, as an equal, you know?"

Mrs. Murray nodded. "Southern women have had Negro domestic help for many generations. It's part of the culture in the South, and not something that will change easily."

"I know, but, well that's not the only thing. When I was a little girl, around ten, I remember going shopping with my mother in Jackson. We went into a nice ladies' store downtown, and while we were shopping a Negro woman came in the front door. She was nicely dressed and very attractive. But one of the White clerks in the store—I think she might have been the store manager—saw her and yelled at her. Her face was so angry and mean."

"What did she say?"

"I don't like to repeat it, but she said, 'Get out of our store, nigger!' I couldn't believe it. I had never heard anyone be so cruel before. I guess I've had a pretty sheltered life."

"I can see how that could have made you more sensitive to racial issues."

"Yes, and during junior high and high school when the Civil Rights Movement became so big in Jackson, I tried to do something to help. I wrote articles for our high school paper, and I tried to talk to my parents and my friends about what was happening, but none of them wanted to have anything to do with it."

"That's not surprising. Most people don't want to get involved. They don't want change—some are even afraid of it. What do your parents think about John?"

"They—they don't know."

"They don't know you are dating him?"

"No, ma'am. I've been afraid to tell them. And now they are sure to hear about what happened tonight and they will be furious with me. Isn't that ironic? They should be furious at those stupid boys who attacked John."

"Sounds like you've got a big decision to make. Why don't you get some sleep now and think about it some more tomorrow?"

When Mary Margaret got to her room, her friend Carol Ann was waiting for her, along with Shannon. They both looked at her and then each other, waiting for someone to break the silence. It was Shannon.

"Are you okay?"

Mary Margaret sat on her bed, across from her friends who were both sitting on Shannon's bed. She took her shoes off and scooted back on the bed, crossing her legs. Letting out a sigh, she looked at Carol Ann.

"I'm fine, but no thanks to you."

Carol Ann hung her head.

"It wasn't her fault," Shannon said.

"No, but she didn't do anything to help." Mary Margaret couldn't stop the tears that had been building. She wanted to be angry, but her anger was mingled with pain and disappointment.

"What could I have done?" Carol Ann said. "You know what Jimbo is like, especially when he's been drinking."

"Of course you're going to stick up for him. You and most of my sorority sisters who just watched John getting beat up and walked on by. Please, just leave."

Carol Ann got up and walked out, leaving Mary Margaret alone with Shannon.

"You know, I warned you about this the first time John visited you here at the house."

"I know. And I know that you were raised just like I was, or maybe with even more racial prejudice coming up in the Delta in a family who made their fortune on the backs of slaves."

"That's not fair." Shannon sat up on the edge of her bed, closer to Mary Margaret. "And that was generations ago. All my daddy's workers are hired, like his daddy's before him."

Mary Margaret climbed off her bed and walked over to her closet to undress and change into pajamas. Pulling her hair up into a bun, she picked up her toiletry bucket and headed out the door to the bathroom down the hall. Turning back to Shannon she said, "I guess that's what you have to tell yourself so you can accept your family. I get that. But we're not on the plantation here at Ole Miss. Or are we?"

John called the next day and asked if Mary Margaret would meet him at the Grove to talk. It was Sunday morning, and the Grove was almost empty, as most students were sleeping in after the football game and a night of parties. One or two kids walked by, glancing at them but not stopping. As they sat on the grass under one of the tall oak trees, an early fall breeze tempered the thick heat and humidity. A few orange and yellow leaves floated down from the tree as they searched one another's eyes and hearts. John had a bruise on his left cheek. Mary Margaret reached to touch it gently, wanting to kiss it but holding back. Finally, she spoke the words that had kept her up all night.

"I am so sorry for what happened. I tried to talk to Carol Ann when I got inside the house, but she stood up for Jimbo."

"Of course she did." John shrugged and looked away.

"And I don't think it's going to stop if we keep seeing each other."

"I know. And I don't want to ruin your life. This is my battle, not yours."

"But it should be everyone's battle, shouldn't it?"

"Yes, but there's a time for everything, and maybe it's not my time yet. It took a hundred and fourteen years for Blacks to be admitted here, and look at the war that caused. I'm going to keep fighting, Mary Margaret. But I understand if this isn't what you want to do. Your family, your friends, your future—they are all waiting for you to resume your life."

John's eyes filled with tears and Mary Margaret fell into his arms. They held their embrace until Mary Margaret pulled away and stood. She couldn't find the words she so desperately wanted. John stood and their eyes met one more time before they walked away in opposite directions.

John and Mary Margaret only saw each other in English class for the rest of the semester. John hung out with his friends more often, making plans with other Black students to organize the Black Student Union (BSU). Mary Margaret poured herself into social activities hosted by the fraternities and sororities on campus, and accepted invitations to ball games and parties from several different boys. The end of the semester was bittersweet, as she headed home to spend the Christmas holidays with her family. She had arranged her schedule for second semester so that she wouldn't be in class with John when she returned. She knew seeing him in class would stoke her feelings for him. It would be too painful.

The challenge to writers today, I think, is not to disown any part of our heritage.

—Eudora Welty

CHAPTER 5

Christmas Break (1966-67)
Mary Margaret

Being back in her childhood home after her first semester in a sorority house brought surprises to Mary Margaret. First, it was the way her parents treated her—especially her mother. While Mary Margaret felt that she had grown up quite a bit in her first months at Ole Miss, her mother seemed oblivious, insisting on treating her like the child she no longer was. Mary Margaret had become accustomed to coming and going without having to account for every action and destination.

"Bye, Mom. See you tonight," she called to her mother from the front door as she was leaving the house early one afternoon. Her mother hurried to intercept her.

"Where are you going?"

"Out."

"Out where?"

"I don't know, Mom. Just out. Do I have to tell you every detail about my life?"

Just then a horn honked and Mary Margaret turned and headed

towards a bright red Ford Mustang at the end of their front sidewalk, driven by a handsome boy with sandy hair. He got out of the car and opened the door for Mary Margaret, turning to wave at her mother.

"Hello, Mrs. Sutherland!"

Her mother's expression changed as she saw that it was Adam Wentworth, Mary Margaret's high school friend who played basketball at State.

"Oh, hi, Adam! How are your parents?"

"They're fine. I'll tell them you asked about them."

Mary Margaret hopped into the car and waved at her mother—almost dismissively—as they drove away.

"My mother thinks I'm still a child. She expects me to tell her everything I'm doing every minute of every day," she said, with a note of exasperation in her voice.

Adam laughed. "Cut her some slack. You're her baby, and you've only been away at college for a few months. My parents did the same thing to my sister."

His words relaxed her, just as his presence always had during the years of their friendship.

It was a sunny but chilly December afternoon, so Adam kept the roof up on his convertible. They were meeting up at the bowling alley with some other friends from high school, including Betsy Lawrence, who was also a freshman at Ole Miss. Betsy had always had a crush on Adam and resented his friendship with Mary Margaret. She had pledged Delta Gamma, so she and Mary Margaret didn't see much of each other at college, as their sororities kept them busy with separate social activities. But Betsy had obviously heard about John Abbott, and didn't waste much time asking about him.

While everyone was sitting around the snack counter after bowling a couple of games, Betsy brought up the topic Mary Margaret was dreading, speaking loudly enough for everyone to hear.

"So, what did your parents think about what happened at school with you and John—what's his last name?"

Adam and the others looked at Mary Margaret, waiting for her answer.

"His name is John Abbott, and they haven't mentioned it."

"You mean, you haven't told them?" Betsy asked.

"Told them what?" Adam said.

"John is a boy from Memphis I dated briefly this fall, if you can call it dating. We only went out once, and that was to a football game. Mostly we were just friends and studied together some. We met in English class and he's super smart and we both love Faulkner and—" suddenly she realized she was talking fast and saying too much, hurrying to explain herself.

"Um, aren't you leaving something out?" Betsy asked, looking at Mary Margaret with a face that said, *Gotcha*!

"Why don't you just say it, Betsy, since it's obviously such a big deal to you."

Betsy looked around at their friends and then back at Mary Margaret with a smug expression. "I think the big deal is the fact that the boy is a Negro."

Silence fell on the group until Adam finally spoke. "A Negro? You dated a Negro? When were you going to tell me about this?"

"Why should I need to tell you everything about my life at Ole Miss, Adam? It's not like you and I are dating or anything."

"So, what happened . . . with John?" another friend asked.

Mary Margaret took a deep breath and tried to slow her words. "We were walking back to the Tri Delt house one night after the football game, and some idiots started picking on him. Calling him names. And hitting him. They punched him in the face and knocked him to the ground, and then kicked him."

"How awful," Adam said, his irritation subsiding. "What happened after that?"

"We agreed that it wasn't going to work so we never saw each other again. Oh, except for in English class, but that's over now that the semester has ended."

The group of friends said their goodbyes and Adam and Mary Margaret got into his car.

"I can't believe your parents don't know," Adam said.

"I know. I was dreading their response, so please don't tell them, or your parents either, since your mom would surely tell mine."

Adam drove Mary Margaret home in silence, dropping her off in front of her house without getting out of the car to open her door. She ran into the house and to her room without speaking to her mother, hoping for some privacy, a place where she could release the tears that she had been holding back.

The next day she decided to visit Eudora Welty. She was a little embarrassed that she hadn't been back to see her since their visits back in the summer of 1963. She hadn't wanted to intrude, and of course Mary Margaret's own high school years had been filled with all the usual activities of a privileged White girl in Jackson, Mississippi. But her experience with John Abbott had changed something inside her, and she felt drawn back to Miss Welty's house again. She knocked on the front door one mid-afternoon, carrying a small fruitcake her mother had made.

Miss Welty opened the door and a smile spread across her face. "Mary Margaret! What a nice surprise. It's been a long time. Please come in."

Mary Margaret handed her the fruitcake. "It's from my mother—one of her holiday traditions. Hope you like it."

"I love it. In fact, let's have some now, with some tea. Or do you prefer coffee?"

"Tea will be fine, thanks."

Sitting again in the cozy sunroom on the back of Miss Welty's house, Mary Margaret felt warm and safe.

"Tell me all about school," Miss Welty began. "You're in college now, aren't you?"

"Yes, ma'am. I'm a freshman at Ole Miss."

"Ole Miss. Wonderful. I hope you're taking advantage of the

Faulkner room at the library there."

"Oh, yes ma'am. And I did a paper about *The Sound and the Fury* for my English class this semester." Talking about the paper and the class primed Mary Margaret to raise what she really wanted to talk about.

"I met a boy who loves literature as much as I do. We studied together and became good friends, but then—" Tears welled and Miss Welty picked up a box of tissues and carried it to Mary Margaret, placing it on the coffee table and sitting next to her on the loveseat.

"Oh, my. I feel a story coming on. Do you want to talk about it?"

Mary Margaret nodded, wiped her nose with the tissue, and told Miss Welty all about John Abbott. About their times studying together. About their date. About the harassment. And finally about how they broke up.

"Do your parents know?" Miss Welty asked.

"No!" she blurted, to Miss Welty's surprise. "I am so sorry. It's just that everyone keeps asking me that. I'm hoping they don't find out. It would just cause problems. I haven't seen John in some time, so I just don't see any reason to bring it up. I'm trying to move on, but—"

"But, what?"

"It's just not fair, the way Negroes are treated, is it?"

"It certainly is not. But this isn't a new problem. It's been going on since the days of slavery, especially here in the South. And I'm afraid it's not going to change without many years of struggles. White people aren't eager to let go of the way of life they've experienced, and they are afraid of what will happen if Negroes are treated as their equals."

"What do they think will happen?"

"Well, for one thing, many White people believe that Negroes are intellectually inferior. They don't want them to gain power politically because they don't believe they are capable of governing wisely."

"That's stupid! John was the smartest person in our English class, and he plans to go to law school."

"Yes, but before you met John and got to know him, what was

your general impression of Negroes?"

"I guess I didn't have much of one. Our maid doesn't have any formal education, and there weren't any Negroes in my schools growing up, so I never really thought much about it."

"Well, it's good that you're thinking about it now. And if you still want to be a writer, you will have a voice for sharing your opinions."

Mary Margaret blew her nose and reached for her tea, beginning to relax.

"Are you still writing about civil rights issues? I remember that short story you wrote when Medgar Evers was murdered."

"Yes, I'm working on another story right now, as a matter of fact. I'm calling it "The Demonstrators."

"Oh, is it about Negroes demonstrating to get equal treatment?"

"Somewhat. There are civil rights demonstrators in it—some Negro and some White—but it's more subtle than a newspaper story. The tone—tone is everything in writing, you know—it's actually kind of gentle. It's about relationships, and the assault of hope that keeps us going in the midst of tragic situations."

"Oh, I can't wait to read it."

"Did you do any writing for your classes this first semester?"

"Not short stories. Only essay questions on exams. Oh, and I write articles for our newspaper, *The Daily Mississippian*."

"Oh, that's wonderful. Now there's an opportunity to find your voice."

"Yes, ma'am. I hope so. Well, I've got to get home. Mother has arranged a busy social calendar for me during the holidays. Thank you so much for the tea and the conversation."

"You are more than welcome. Please come again."

Mary Margaret had stopped crying and was caught up in the beauty of Miss Welty's language. She had almost forgotten about her own situation.

Walking back home after her visit, she realized that she still had feelings for John, and she felt guilty for not having the courage to stay with him. But she also felt that she wasn't equipped to go to war with her family and the society she was raised in. And that society presented itself with glitz and glamour—and societal expectations reinforced by her mother—especially during the Christmas holidays.

"Ready to go shopping?" her mother asked Mary Margaret a few days later. Mrs. Sutherland was dressed to the nines for their day together, in her black and white tweed Christian Dior suit. "Oh—you're not wearing that, are you?"

Mary Margaret had on ankle pants and a baggy pullover sweater. "We're just going shopping. Why do I have to get dressed up?"

"A young lady should always look her best while shopping. Besides, we're meeting Mrs. Lawrence and Betsy for lunch at Primos. Didn't Betsy tell you? Now go put on that cute corduroy jumper and do something with your hair."

Mary Margaret's stomach sank when her mother mentioned Betsy. Dot Lawrence was one of her mother's best friends. Had Betsy told her mother about John? Their fun day of shopping was suddenly shrouded with a dark cloud. Should she tell her mother now and avoid the possible drama at lunch, or take her chances that Betsy hadn't told? She decided to wait and hope for the best.

After a morning at all their favorite stores, which Mary Margaret noticed were devoid of any Negro shoppers, they arrived at Primos for lunch. Owned by a prominent Jackson family, Primos was always full of the society crowd, and today was no exception. Seated at a table with Betsy and their mothers, she ordered a chicken salad sandwich and sweet tea. She picked at her food as they talked, worried that Betsy would spill the beans, if she hadn't already.

"Well, isn't this lovely?" Mrs. Lawrence said.

"Yes, how wonderful to have our little girls home for the holidays and for all of us to be together again," Mary Margaret's mother said.

"You girls are unusually quiet," Mrs. Lawrence said, looking at Betsy and Mary Margaret.

"Oh, yes ma'am. Just tired from the all-night study sessions during exams, I guess," Mary Margaret answered.

"I'm sure you'll make the Dean's list," Betsy said. "It seems like you're always studying when I see you in the library or at the Grove at school." She trained her eyes on Mary Margaret, who feared the worst was coming.

"Well, the Tri Delts put a lot of pressure on freshmen to do well academically," Mary Margaret countered, "as I'm sure the Delta Gammas do."

"My goodness, so much talk about studying and grades," Mrs. Sutherland said. "What about your social lives? Do you girls ever see each other at parties and such?"

"Not really," Betsy was quick to answer, "especially since we're in different sororities, and the boys we've dated aren't in the same fraternity."

"That's too bad," Mrs. Sutherland said. "Y'all were such good friends in high school. Well, I'm glad you're having some time together over the holidays."

"Yes," Mrs. Lawrence said, "y'all went bowling the other day, right? With Adam Wentworth and some of your other pals?"

Mary Margaret shot a pleading look at Betsy and held her breath.

"Yes, that was fun," Betsy said. "In fact, Adam and I have had a couple of dates since then." Betsy's triumphant smile told Mary Margaret that she was going to settle for this victory and not rat her out to her mother.

Mary Margaret mouthed a quick *thank you* and said, "Oh, that's wonderful. You and Adam make a great couple."

The rest of lunch and the afternoon of more shopping passed without incident, and Mary Margaret was so exhausted when they got home that she crashed on her bed for a nap. That evening was spent listening to Christmas music while wrapping gifts with her mother, who was a master gift wrapper. Her brother Billy had moved back into the house from his dorm on the Millsaps campus where he was a junior. Their father had done his customary duty of bringing home the six-foot balsam fir and stringing it with lights. Mary Margaret and Billy trimmed the tree while their mother made homemade divinity, another family tradition Mary Margaret much preferred to fruitcakes. Everything was picture perfect. For now.

To accept one's past—one's history—is not the same thing as drowning in it;
it is learning how to use it.

—**James Baldwin,** *The Fire Next Time*

CHAPTER 6

Christmas Break (1966-67)
John

John wasn't as successful as Mary Margaret in keeping their secret from his parents. It wasn't that anyone ratted him out. It was his own conscience that betrayed him. He had always worn his feelings on his sleeve, and his father, despite his tough exterior, had a second sense about his son and could usually tell when something was bothering John. One night after supper he and his father were sitting in the den while his mother was in the kitchen, poring over recipes for Christmas dinner.

"You're mighty quiet tonight, John," his father said.

"Oh, sorry. Just tired I guess."

"You sure there's not more to it? Everything okay at school? I know I was tough on you about going to Ole Miss, but now that you're there, I want you to be happy. Anything going on that I need to know about?"

John's mother came in from the kitchen and joined them, picked up a shirt from a basket near her chair and began to sew on a missing button. She smiled at John, and listened quietly.

"No. I mean my grades are good and I like the classes. Especially English." As soon as he mentioned English class, he knew he would have to tell them about Mary Margaret. "But, well, I met a girl in class who loves Faulkner as much as I do, and we started studying together after class."

His mother looked up from her sewing with a broad smile. "You met a girl?" The eagerness in her face nearly broke John's heart. He always hated to disappoint his mother.

"Yes, but, well—" John hung his head, ashamed of what he was about to say. There was no way out of it. So he told his parents about what happened—playing down the assault that left him bloodied and humiliated. He was sure his dad would have wanted him to fight back.

His dad stood and walked around the room as John spoke. Finally he said, "You went on a date with a White girl? A rich White girl who lives in one of those sorority houses? What on earth were you thinking?"

"We agreed to stop seeing each other after that, so what's the big deal?"

"The *big deal* is that you could get in a bunch of trouble and maybe even get kicked out of that swanky school, not that I wanted you to go there in the first place. But now that you're there, you better be careful if you hope to get that degree and have a chance at law school."

John thought about Eddie and Dianna and his other friends in Ole Miss' Black Student Union who met to discuss civil rights issues on campus. He couldn't promise his father that he was going to fly under the radar when it came to social injustice.

"I hear you, Dad, but the whole reason I'm going to school and want to be a lawyer is so I can fight for justice for our people."

"I understand that, son, but you'll never get the chance if you get kicked out of school. Just be careful, that's all I'm saying."

John looked at his mother, who sat quietly but begged him with her eyes. He nodded at both of them before leaving the room. Thoughts of Mary Margaret flooded his mind as he unpacked in his room, surrounded by memories of high school—athletic trophies and photographs of him with dates at dances. Not a white face anywhere to be found.

Hanging out with his brother Frank during the holidays reminded him of the other life he could be living if he had accepted a football scholarship to TSU and remained in the social circles he grew up in. Everywhere they went they were flocked by friends who admired them. Frank was popular and happy-go-lucky. John couldn't help but be a little jealous, watching his older brother move so comfortably in the world of his upbringing.

Getting milkshakes at a drive-in hamburger joint one day, Frank asked John, "So, are you happy at Ole Miss? Do you miss football?"

"Yes. And yes. It's different, that's for sure. But it will be worth it when I get to law school, and someday when I'm practicing law here in Memphis."

"That's cool," Frank said. "But just remember that the climb up that ladder ain't going to be easy."

One night at a local club John hooked up with a group of high school friends, including his best friend George and his old girlfriend Jacqueline, who looked prettier than ever. He was immediately the center of attention, with everyone wanting to talk with him and the girls all wanting to dance. It felt good to be back with his people, and for one evening he questioned his decision to attend Ole Miss—until later that night when everything changed.

John wasn't a drinker, but George was and couldn't hold his liquor. So John insisted he drive him home. On the way to George's house, he saw blue lights in his rearview mirror and heard a police siren. He looked at his dashboard to be sure he wasn't speeding; he was only going thirty in a thirty-five zone. Pulling over, he looked at George who had passed out in the passenger seat. That wasn't going to go well. Two White policemen approached his car. He rolled down his window and looked at the officer and spoke politely.

"Good evening, sir. Is there a problem?" His father had taught him to always be polite to cops.

The policeman looked into the car and saw George. "What's wrong with your friend?"

"I'm afraid he had a bit too much to drink, so I'm driving him home."

"Step out of the car, boy," the policeman gruffly insisted.

John did as he was told.

"You been drinking, too?"

"No, sir. Nothing but soda."

The policeman made John walk in a straight line, which he did without faltering. The other cop with him said, "Come on, Robert. Looks like the boy didn't do anything wrong. Let's just let him go with a warning."

"Shut up, Larry. You're just a rookie. Watch and learn."

"Turn around, boy. Hands on the car." The policeman frisked John, and finding nothing, he told his partner to search the car. "I'm sure you'll find some booze or drugs in there."

But he found nothing in the car, and by that time George was awake and confused about what was happening.

"John!" he yelled. "What's going on?"

"Shut up, George. Just do what they tell you."

"Pull him out and cuff him," the first officer told the rookie. Then he cuffed John. When the other officer pulled George out of the car, George puked all over him. The first officer put John in the squad car and then walked over to where George and the rookie were standing, both covered in vomit. "Damn it, Larry. Can't you do anything right?" Then he pushed George to the ground and kicked him twice. George groaned and didn't move. Finally, Robert shouted at him to get up, but he was unable to stand on his own. "Take his sorry ass to the squad car," Robert shouted at the rookie cop. "And you're going to clean the car later!"

In the squad car John heard Robert tell Larry, "I'm sure these boys are both minors. This'll teach 'em a lesson."

At the police station John called his father, who came rushing from home. He asked the clerk at the desk, "This won't be on his record, will it?"

The clerk, who happened to be Black, looked at some paperwork. "It says DUI here." He looked at John. "Were you drinking?"

"No, sir. I told the officer I wasn't, and I passed the sobriety test. I was driving my friend home."

The clerk paused for a minute, and then looked over his shoulder and around the room. He marked something on the document and said, "This never happened, you hear me, brother? But you be careful out there."

"Thank you so much . . . and what about George?"

"He was pretty drunk, but since he wasn't driving, he'll probably get off pretty easy."

On the drive home, John's father was unusually quiet. Finally, he spoke.

"Do you have any idea how lucky you were tonight? If that had been a White clerk, you'd have a DUI on your record, and you could kiss your college education goodbye. Not to mention law school."

"But I wasn't doing anything wrong, Dad. I wasn't drinking or speeding, and I was polite to the officer, like you taught me. What am I supposed to do, just stay home all the time?"

No one spoke the rest of the drive home, but John's mind was anything but quiet. When they got to the house his father said, "Your mother is asleep. She doesn't need to know anything about this. Just get to bed quietly."

John couldn't sleep, with thoughts of events like this happening to Negro teenagers—and even adults—with no way to defend themselves. His resolve to become a lawyer strengthened, but his fears of making it through the coming years intensified.

The rest of the holidays were uneventful, and Christmas day brought lots of relatives crammed into their modest house, and an abundance of their favorite foods, including turkey and Southern cornbread dressing, homemade biscuits, and his mother's famous buttermilk pie. Opening presents was never the center of the holiday for his family—they couldn't afford expensive gifts. Christmas day was more about celebrating what they did have and not focusing on what was missing. But John couldn't help but think about what—or who—he was missing as he watched his parents embrace and smile at their family gathered together in peace.

Never be afraid to raise your voice for honesty and truth and compassion against injustice and lying and greed. If people all over the world . . . would do this, it would change the earth.

—William Faulkner

CHAPTER 7

Ole Miss (1967-70)

Once they returned to Ole Miss from Christmas break, John and Mary Margaret continued with their separate lives on campus. Somehow, they managed not to have any classes together for the rest of their semesters. As they focused their attention on different interests, their social and cultural activities became more polarized. Mary Margaret's life centered on finishing her degree in Education and preparing for her future life as a teacher, as well as a new romance and sorority life. John's involvement in civil rights issues intensified.

By the second semester of their sophomore year, John had become closer with his friends Eddie and Dianna. One day at lunch in March of 1968, Eddie asked John what he knew about the sanitation workers' strike that had started in Memphis in February.

"Two men were crushed to death by a malfunctioning truck," John began. "The city wasn't doing anything about it, so over a thousand workers went on strike a couple of weeks later. And it wasn't just about the death of those two workers. It was also about their wages being so low that many are on welfare and food stamps just to feed their families."

"I heard the police used mace and tear gas against peaceful protesters at City Hall," Eddie said.

"Yeah, my dad was there. He said the protests have continued, and a bunch of high school and college kids—even White kids—have joined in."

"You going up there to participate?" Dianna asked.

"Maybe. You know Dr. King was there last week. Spoke to a crowd of about 25,000. Since then, the striking workers have been carrying signs saying 'I Am a Man.' I heard he was going to return to Memphis on April 3 to speak again."

"Let's go!" Eddie said, standing and raising his fist in the air.

"I'm in!" Dianna said.

Eddie and Dianna looked at John, waiting for him to join their enthusiastic cry.

"I don't know," John said. "Gotta' think about it. See y'all tomorrow."

John was struggling with his feelings. With two papers due soon and exams just around the corner, he wasn't sure it was the best thing for him to do. Should he join the protesters in Memphis or stay at school and continue to work towards his long-term goals? What if he got arrested? Unable to sleep that night, he called his father, waking him around midnight.

"John? You okay?"

"Hi, Dad. Yeah, I'm fine. Well, not *fine*, but I'm not hurt or anything. I just couldn't sleep thinking about everything happening in Memphis right now. Some of my friends here are thinking about coming up to join the protests. We hear Dr. King might be returning to Memphis soon. What do you think?"

"Son, I know you're anxious to get involved, but it's dangerous. And if you get arrested, there goes your chance at law school and the important things you got planned for the future."

John nodded on the other end of the call.

"You still there?" his dad asked.

"Yeah. I'm just so frustrated. But I know you're right. Eddie and some other kids will probably drive up soon."

"You stay put, you hear me?"

"I hear you, Dad."

Of course, what John missed by not going to Memphis was Dr. King's famous speech, "I've Been to the Mountaintop," which he gave at Bishop Charles Mason Temple on April 3, 1968. And when John heard that Dr. King had talked about "dangerous unselfishness" and encouraged students to leave school and join the protests, he was even more conflicted. When Dr. King was assassinated the next day on the balcony of the Lorraine Motel, John decided to drive to Memphis.

On April 8, John—with his father by his side—joined 42,000 others, led by Coretta Scott King and union leaders on a peaceful march through Memphis to City Hall, demanding justice for the sanitation workers. It was an experience he would never forget. He was so proud of his father and the other men for their conviction and courage, and maybe for the first time in his life he felt himself to be a man. To be one of them. He envisioned himself practicing law in Memphis one day, or even becoming a judge. He longed for the power that would provide for his future work defending the rights of his people.

He returned to school the next day, and a week later he heard the news that negotiators had reached a deal with the City Council to recognize the union and guarantee a better wage. The strike was over. And although it would take months—and another strike threatened by the union—the city finally followed through with its commitment.

"Aren't you glad you were there?" Eddie asked John on their way to meet Dianna at the student union the next day.

"Oh, man, yes! And I'm even gladder I didn't get arrested. Now I gotta' keep studying and hopefully make it to law school, so I can get back to Memphis in a few years with a law degree under my belt."

"You gonna' do it, brother!"

By senior year, Mary Margaret was practice teaching at a local high school and had begun dating a senior from Memphis named Walker Richardson. Walker was everything her mother wished for her—tall, handsome, popular, and with a secure future in his father's property development and management business. She was wearing his Sigma Chi pin and hoping for a ring before graduation. She was even chosen as the Sweetheart of Sigma Chi, an honor envied by girls all over the campus. Walker and his fraternity brothers serenaded her outside the Tri Delt house one night, where he presented her with roses and the brothers sang the song popular since 1913:

The girl of my dreams is the sweetest girl
Of all the girls I know
And the moon still beams
On the girl of my dreams
She's the sweetheart of Sigma Chi.

But even as she was caught up in the magic of the serenade and the honor of being the Sweetheart of Sigma Chi, Mary Margaret cringed a little bit inside, realizing that she was in love with the *idea* of Walker and the future he promised more than with Walker, the *person*. Even his kisses lacked some of the passion she hoped for.

Although her mother was happy for her, she wished that her daughter's potential husband were a Jackson boy. She wanted to keep Mary Margaret close to home where she could continue to shape her and get her involved in Junior League and the other social activities that mattered. The two young people weren't engaged yet, but it seemed inevitable.

Even after what happened with George and the policemen in Memphis during the holidays, and the King assassination, John became even more active in the Black Student Union, which he had helped to form. The group wasn't violent in nature. Their first demonstration was at the college cafeteria, in February of 1970, where a group of forty took over separate tables, each one of them dancing to Eldridge Cleaver's cry for Black Power as strains of "Soul on Wax" exploded from a record player. Most of the White students just stared at them, or left quietly. But Eddie noticed one boy sitting at a table alone, so he took his tray and sat down with him. The White kid shouted at him, "You can't sit here, boy! Get away from my table!"

John listened from a nearby table and said, "What do you mean he can't sit there? We can sit wherever we want!" He joined Eddie at the table. Soon others saw what was happening and sat with them. The White student stood without eating and said, "Fuck this shit," and left. The Black students all laughed and applauded.

John stood up on top of the table and started speaking. Quoting the Freedom Democratic Party advocate, Mississippi native Fannie Lou Hamer, John said, "I'm sick and tired of being sick and tired."

Dianna went to the bookstore and got a Confederate flag. She brought it back to the cafeteria and set it on fire. John turned off the music and all the students watched it burn in silence.

Next, a few of the students, including John, Eddie, and Dianna, went to the campus security office and filed over forty complaints against the university. Many detailed specific grievances, but most had the words *RACIAL DISCRIMINATION* written at the top in all capital letters.

The Black Student Union had already sent a list of twenty-seven demands to Chancellor Porter Fortune—who had actually permitted the formation of the BSU so that Black students would have a venue for expressing their concerns about the acts of harassment towards Blacks and the inequality in the student body, faculty, and staff at the university. The concerns included the fact that Blacks weren't allowed to play on athletic teams. There were still fewer than 200 Black students at a school of over 7,000. Not getting a response to their demands, they discussed what to do next.

"Fortune ain't listening to us," said Eddie.

"He's always polite," John said.

"Yeah, but polite ain't getting our demands answered," said Dianna.

"Let's take it to the man," said Eddie.

"What do you mean?" asked John.

"Let's pay him a visit at home."

Chancellor Fortune's home was on campus, right across the street from the old law school building. About forty Black students went to his house that night and gathered on his large front porch. They knocked on the front door over and over for about thirty minutes. Finally, he opened the door.

"How can I help you boys and girls?"

"You can put an end to racial discrimination on campus," John said. "Didn't you get the demands we sent you?"

"Yes, I got them, but it takes times to get things done. All of your complaints will be answered."

The students started shouting and one boy made a move to hit the Chancellor, but other students held him back. Several people yelled, "Don't hit him!" Another student shouted out, "Look up! Look up!" He was pointing to the third floor of the building across the street, where several highway patrolmen had guns pointed at the students.

John realized then why it had taken the chancellor so long to answer the door—he was calling in the patrolmen. Fortunately, everyone left peacefully without arrests. But tempers were ignited. Another opportunity would present itself the next day.

John and his friends went to another BSU meeting the following evening.

"Have y'all heard about the musical group 'Up With People' that's performing at Fulton Chapel tonight?" Dianna was often the first to speak at their meetings.

"Yeah, so what?" Eddie asked.

"Well, I was thinking that would be a good place to protest, since they claim to be all about peace and unity. Maybe we could even storm the stage during the concert."

"What good would that do?" John asked, surprised by Dianna's suggestion.

"You know, I was just thirteen when Meredith came on campus and turned Oxford upside down. I was watching from behind some bushes with some of my friends until the Guard showed up. That was some scary shit. Imagine the courage it took for him to do that. We've got to do something."

"I think I heard that some reporters will be at the concert," Eddie said.

"Now we're getting somewhere," John agreed. "We need some publicity. Let's do this."

When they arrived at the event two White students were at the door. John said, "We're here to protest racial discrimination at Ole Miss. Let us inside." The White students saw that there were over sixty Black students in line behind them, so they stepped aside and let them in.

John, Eddie, Dianna, and the other Black students calmly walked up the aisles and onto the stage. During Up With People's song, "What Color is God's Skin," Eddie grabbed the microphone and began to speak. Then someone turned the power off. A student in the crowd shouted, "The police are outside! The building is surrounded!" The whole group peacefully walked out of the chapel and into the flashing lights of sixty or seventy police cruisers. Highway Patrol cars. More Black students had rushed to Fulton Chapel to join their friends, and sixty-one students were arrested, including John, Eddie and Dianna.

Luckily, the three of them were sent to the local jail, unlike many who were sent to Parchman, the state's maximum security prison. And although all the students who were taken to the county jail were released the next day, eight of them, including Dianna, were expelled. John and Eddie were lucky the charges were dropped against them, which would have ruined John's chances at law school, and possibly

Eddie's dream of becoming a college professor.

"What happened with Dianna?" Eddie asked John after they heard about her punishment. "How come she got expelled and we didn't?"

"I think it's because she told them the protest was her idea," John said.

"Wow, that woman has guts."

Back at their dorm later, John asked Eddie, "So, what are your plans after graduation? Have you applied for grad school yet?"

"Yep. In math. So I can teach college level. Hoping to hear soon. You?"

"Same here. Still waiting to hear from the law school. And hoping this incident doesn't blow my chances."

"I was thinking you might end up leaving the state for law school," Eddie said. "You sure you want to stay in this environment?"

"The reason I want to be a lawyer is to get in a better position to change things," John said. "Leaving Mississippi isn't the answer for me."

"Me, neither."

John and Eddie exchanged a *dap*—the Black Power handshake that stood for Dignity And Pride. That's how John was trying to live his life.

The next day, *The Daily Mississippian* featured a photograph of eight student protesters on the stage at the concert, several with fists raised in Black Power salutes. The headline read, "Eighty-nine Negros Arrested." Dianna was visible in the picture. A group of White student leaders sent a letter to the editor, pointing out how severe the punishment was for peaceful acts of protest by Black students, compared with little or no punishment for destruction of property or for the fireworks that White students threw into passing cars during parties on Fraternity Row. John's name was listed among those arrested.

"Did you see the article about John and his friends in *The Daily Mississippian*?" Mrs. Murray asked Mary Margaret after lunch one day at the sorority house.

"Yes ma'am. Wasn't that a great letter the White students wrote?"

"Indeed it was."

"I really wish I had signed it. Or even known about it." Mary Margaret was no longer on the newspaper staff. She had become less involved in politics and was spending more time dreaming about summer vacation at the beach . . . and a wedding.

"Do you regret your decision? John seems to be growing into a fine man. I can see him making a difference—a real change for his people. For all of us."

Mary Margaret thought about her answer for a minute. "Yes and no. I think I'll always be ambivalent about it. And a bit disappointed in myself for not having the courage of my convictions."

Mrs. Murray gave her a hug. "You are a special young woman. Keep your heart open. There's no telling what the future will bring."

"Maybe so, but for now everything seems to be lining up just the way my parents—especially my mother—hoped."

"Oh? Are you expecting a proposal from Walker soon?"

"I sure hope so!"

A few weeks later, a candle decorated with fresh flowers arrived at the Tri Delt house from a local florist. There was no name on the delivery, but Mrs. Murray understood its meaning. She placed the candle on a table in the foyer, where it was visible to all the girls as they came and went from the front door or the stairs leading to their rooms. Giggles and whispers filled the dining room at dinner that night, and afterwards the chapter president stood and made the announcement.

"As I'm sure everyone has noticed, we will be having a candlelight service after dinner in the chapter room."

A candlelight was a long-standing tradition among most sororities, and Delta Delta Delta was no exception. When a member of the sorority was dropped, pinned, or engaged to a fraternity member, she ordered a decorated candle delivered to the house. She kept her secret until the ceremony, during which a special sorority song was sung as the sisters stood in a circle, passing the lit candle around. If the sorority member announced that she has been dropped—received a small fraternity emblem on a necklace, indicating that the couple is dating—she blew the candle out the first time it came to her in the ceremony. If she announced that she received her boyfriend's fraternity pin to wear, indicating a more serious relationship, she blew the candle out the second time it came around. And if she was announcing her engagement, she waited until its third time around the room to blow the candle out.

Mary Margaret stood next to Shannon and Carol Ann—whose friendships had survived despite their differences—and smiled at them nervously, trying not to give anything away. Once the chapter president lit the candle and the song began, all the giggles subsided and anticipation filled the room. Their voices rang out with the song they knew so well.

"A Tri Delt girl is like a melody . . ."

Mary Margaret's tummy was doing somersaults, but she had to wait until the third time the candle made its way around the circle.

"That taunts you night and day . . ."

As the candle was passed into her hands the second time, she kept a poker face and passed it on to Carol Ann.

"Just like the strain of a haunting refrain . . ."

She received the candle a third time from Shannon, but just as Carol Ann reached out to take it from her, her face lit up with a revealing smile and she blew it out.

Cheers exploded and everyone in the circle rushed to hug Mary Margaret and asked to see her engagement ring, which she had kept hidden in a pocket during dinner and the ceremony. The white gold setting featured a half-carat center diamond with a smaller one on each side. Gasps and exclamations of "Oh, my gosh!" flooded Mary Margaret all at once. When the crowd quieted, she told everyone the ring had been Walker's great grandmother's, which brought on more exclamations.

"When's the date?" Shannon asked.

"June 13."

"Wow, that's soon," Shannon said.

"Yeah, I've got a lot to do to get ready, especially with exams and graduation coming up."

"Where will y'all live?" another sorority sister asked.

"Memphis. Walker is going to work in his father's property development company, and I'll be teaching at Hutchison in the fall." The Hutchison School for Girls was the most elite private school in Memphis.

Mary Margaret caught Mrs. Murray's eye across the room and noticed her smile, followed by a wink. Yes, her life was proceeding as everyone expected.

Contrary to what his father had told him when he chose to attend Ole Miss for undergraduate studies—and in spite of his participation in the BSU and protests—John found that the all-White faculty liked him. He was especially loved by his political science professor, who admired his ability to see the big picture in any historical setting, and recommended him for acceptance into the university's School of Law for the following year. But he was also lauded by his English professors, who believed his love for literature and grasp of the language would be assets to a future legal career. He graduated Summa Cum Laude and received a rare scholarship for law school.

After the graduation ceremony, John and his parents were walking across the Grove and ran into Mary Margaret and her folks. It was impossible for them to avoid each other, so they exchanged awkward smiles and congratulatory remarks.

"Hi, Mary Margaret," John began. "These are my parents, Richard and Dorothy Abbott. Dad, Mom, this is Mary Margaret Sutherland."

Everyone nodded silently. Mrs. Sutherland shot her daughter a confused look.

"So nice to meet y'all," Mary Margaret said. "My mother and father, Jeanne and David Sutherland. This is John Abbott."

The men exchanged handshakes and the women smiled and nodded.

Mary Margaret tried to cut through the tension. "John and I had an English class together in our freshman year. He's the only one in the class who aced the final exam."

"That's great, John," Mrs. Sutherland said.

"What are your plans now that you've graduated?" Dr. Sutherland asked.

"I've been accepted to law school, sir," John answered.

"With a scholarship," Mr. Abbott added proudly. "What about you, young lady?" he asked Mary Margaret.

"Oh, me? Well, I'm going to teach high school English and literature."

"A teacher? That's wonderful," Mrs. Abbott said. "Where will you be teaching?"

"In Memphis, actually."

John hadn't yet heard Mary Margaret's news and was a bit surprised. "Why Memphis?"

"Well, I'm actually engaged to be married to a boy from Memphis, Walker Richardson. He will be working at his father's property development business, so I got a job teaching school there next year."

Another surprise for John, who couldn't stop himself from asking, "Married? I mean, that's great. A Memphis boy, huh? Where did he go to school?"

"Um, he went to Memphis University School."

John nodded. "When is the wedding?"

"It's actually in a few weeks," Mary Margaret said.

"Congratulations. On your marriage and your teaching career." John struggled to keep his emotions in check.

"Well, we certainly need some good teachers in Memphis," Mrs. Abbott said. "Do you know which school you will be at?"

"I'll be at Hutchison." She felt embarrassed since the Abbotts lived in a Black neighborhood and their boys attended all-Black public schools.

"Those girls will be lucky to have you," John said. "I hope you like Memphis."

"Thank you. Oh, there's Walker's family now!" Mary Margaret waved across the Grove at a group of people who waved back. "Good luck in law school, John."

As both families turned to walk off in opposite directions, John and Mary Margaret both looked over their shoulders for what they assumed would be the last time they would ever see one another.

Back in John and Mary Margaret's kitchen in Harbor Town, they took a break from sharing their story with Adele.

"Oh, my, what an incredible story. I wasn't expecting that." Adele said.

"Yes, it was. It is." John said, looking at Mary Margaret with a slight smile.

"But, wait, it sounds like you two broke up at Ole Miss, and yet here you are—together? And I still don't get what this has to do with Alzheimer's."

Mary Margaret got up to refill their coffee cups. "We're going to need reinforcements. There's a lot more to the story. Are you sure you have time for this?"

"Are you kidding me? I couldn't possibly leave now. You didn't really marry this Walker guy, did you? I have images in my head of John running down the aisle at the wedding to object, like Dustin Hoffman in *The Graduate*, to stop Katharine Ross from marrying Avery." She smiled expectantly at both.

Mary Margaret looked at John but didn't answer Adele's question. Adele quickly filled the awkward silence: "Or maybe it was more like Ryan Gosling and Rachel McAdams in *The Notebook*?" Adele became animated, standing up and walking around, tapping her fingers on the tabletop, her quizzical look intensifying into a frown. Suddenly she turned to Mary Margaret and said, "Oh my gosh, you—you don't have Alzheimer's . . . do you?"

Mary Margaret rose to meet Adele's question face to face, but didn't answer. John followed suit and stood and put his arm on Mary Margaret's shoulder. "I think we should tell her the rest of the story now, don't you?"

"Yes. But let's go into the den where we can get comfortable. This is going to take a while."

Art is never the voice of a country, it is an even more precious thing, the voice of the individual, doing its best to speak, not comfort of any sort, but truth.

—Eudora Welty

CHAPTER 8

Mary Margaret and Walker (1970–2012)

Mary Margaret and Walker's wedding was at First Baptist Church in Jackson, where the Sutherlands had been long-time members. Walker's family came down in droves from Memphis, and the sanctuary overflowed. With eight bridesmaids decked out in pink taffeta and Walker and his eight groomsmen in tails, the only thing more beautiful was Mary Margaret in her mother's mermaid lace gown.

Later at the reception at the Jackson Country Club, Mary Margaret and Walker stood for what felt like hours, receiving socialites and dignitaries. In a rare break between hugs and handshakes, Mary Margaret looked down the receiving line at her parents.

"Oh, no," she said to Walker.

"What's wrong?"

"I can't believe he's here."

"Who?" Walker followed Mary Margaret's eyes, which were homed in on her father and the man he was speaking with.

"Governor Williams."

Walker looked again. "John Bell Williams? That's him? What's he doing here?"

"Oh, he goes to First Baptist, and he's an Ole Miss alum. My father is a big fan."

"So, what's the problem?"

"He's a segregationist."

"Um, so are probably most of the people at this reception. And most of the people in Mississippi—and Memphis, as a matter of fact."

"I know. It's just that I wish he wasn't here. Oh, here he comes."

"You look beautiful, young lady." The governor leaned in for a kiss on her cheek.

"Thank you. Walker, this is Governor Williams."

"It's an honor, sir." Walker offered his hand.

"I hear you're going to be working with your father in his real estate business. Nothing better than family working together."

"I think so, too."

"And your father tells me you're going to be teaching at Hutchison." Governor Williams leaned in to hold Mary Margaret's hands.

"Yes sir. High school English and literature." She pulled her hands away, using one to straighten her hair, trying not to appear repulsed by his touch.

"Sounds like a good plan. By this time next year Memphis public schools are gonna be a mess, thanks to court-ordered integration and busing. Probably gonna happen here in Jackson sooner than that. Some forward-thinking people at East Park Baptist in Memphis are putting together plans for some private schools. Supposed to open in '73 . . . plenty of time for your kids, right?" He poked Walker in the arm and let out a deep laugh.

"Yes sir. Thank you, sir," said Walker, ever the gentleman.

"*Arrggh!* I thought he would never shut up," Mary Margaret whispered to Walker once the governor moved on down the receiving line. "Now you see why I didn't want him here?"

"He is a big windbag, isn't he? But I wouldn't let him bother you.

Pretty soon you will no longer be a resident of his state. We'll make our own lives in Memphis."

After a honeymoon in Hawaii, compliments of Walker's parents, they settled into their first home, a brick bungalow in the Central Gardens neighborhood of Midtown. Mary Margaret loved the neighborhood with its old houses and large front porches where you could visit with your neighbors so easily. They had argued over the choice shortly after their engagement, since it meant a thirty-minute commute to work for Walker. Mary Margaret would have to drive almost that far for her job at Hutchison, but she said she wouldn't mind. She loved Central Gardens, which felt a lot like the Belhaven neighborhood where she grew up back in Jackson. She wasn't in a hurry to live out east.

She won the argument and they enjoyed the early years of their marriage. Mary Margaret loved living near such wonderful literary venues as Burke's Books—the oldest bookstore in Memphis, which had been founded in 1875—and the main library, which was two minutes from their house. As she got to know some of the women on their block, she learned that many of them sent their children to neighborhood public schools, but others chose private schools with long-standing reputations, like nearby Grace-St. Luke's Episcopal, founded in 1947, and St. Mary's Episcopal, the oldest private school in Memphis, founded in 1847. None of their neighbors had girls at Hutchison, where she was teaching, but that might change in the coming years.

Governor Williams had been right about what was going to happen to the public schools in Memphis. Desegregation began in earnest in 1971, and in 1973 the courts ordered the busing of almost 14,000 students, integrating the Memphis City Schools system, which was the tenth largest public school system in the nation. And yet, that same year nearly 8,000 White students left the system. So, the courts came back with another order—this time for almost 40,000 students to be bused, but only 28,000 participated. Another 20,000 Whites left the system for the numerous new private schools that were springing up all over the city. By 1974 Memphis had the largest private segregated school system in the country.

By the end of the 1970s—with the arrival of two daughters and the growing success of the Richardsons' business—they could finally afford the house of Walker's dreams. They joined Walker's parents in the River Oaks neighborhood, just a five-minute drive from Walker's job and about the same distance from their new home to Hutchison, where Mary Margaret continued to teach, and where they planned to enroll their girls. Hutchison wasn't built to keep Blacks out. Founded in 1902, its mission was to give girls a place to succeed academically and explore their creativity. A college prep school on a scenic fifty-two-acre campus, it offered everything Mary Margaret wished she had growing up, and she wanted her own girls to experience what the school had to offer. It did, however, bother her that only a few Black girls attended the school, limiting her daughters' interactions with people of color.

In 1993—twenty years after Mary Margaret began teaching at Hutchison—she became faculty sponsor of the Social Justice Club. It was started by one of the Black students in the upper school to promote awareness of civil rights and social injustice issues in Memphis. Mary Margaret's girls were still in middle school, but she hoped they would join the club once in high school.

One afternoon during a meeting, Dr. Katherine Hanover, head of school at Hutchison, paid a surprise visit to the club. Mary Margaret invited her to speak to the club members.

"I've got wonderful news for you girls," she began. "Next week our guest speaker at assembly will be from the new emergency care center for abused children that's been established at Porter-Leath. It's called Sarah's Place. Most of the children they care for are from underserved families. Many are Black. I know that your club will welcome her and be prepared to ask questions after her talk."

"That's wonderful," said Mary Margaret. "We will be eager to hear her, won't we girls?"

The girls in the club nodded and a few clapped. After Dr. Hanover left, the girls spent the rest of the meeting discussing questions they might like to ask the guest speaker. Mary Margaret was pleased with their enthusiasm.

On the day of the assembly, Mary Margaret and the girls from the club all sat together right down front. Dr. Hanover introduced the speaker and asked the girls to welcome her. Polite applause filled the room and Elizabeth Abbott began. She told the history of Porter-Leath and the services they offer. Then she talked about Sarah's Place. Her love for the children was evident, and the Hutchison girls in the audience were drawn to her. Finally, she asked if there were any questions.

One of the girls in the Social Justice Club was first to speak. "Were you a teenager during the civil rights protests in the 1960s and '70s?"

"Yes, I was. I grew up in Oxford, Mississippi, and I was twelve years old when James Meredith was admitted to Ole Miss. And I was a student at Jackson State during the riot when those students were killed in 1970, just outside my dorm, actually. So when I went to Ole Miss to do graduate work in 1971, I lived with my father away from the campus. He was afraid for me to live on campus."

Several more students asked questions—some about the kids at Sarah's Place, and others about civil rights issues in general. Then a Black girl from the club said, "Hi, Mrs. Abbott. Do you have a son who goes to MUS? I think I met him at a party."

Laughter filled the auditorium.

Elizabeth joined the girls with a laugh. "Yes, I have two boys at MUS, in fact."

The girl continued, "And your husband is Judge John Abbott? Did he really help get NAACP members out of jail back in the day?"

"I can tell my boys have been bragging about their father again," Elizabeth answered. "And yes, that's him."

Mary Margaret suddenly felt flush. *This woman is John Abbott's wife? And they have sons who attend Memphis University School?* Her heart raced and her mind spun back twenty-seven years, to their freshman year at Ole Miss. To those wonderful hours talking about William Faulkner and Eudora Welty. To that kiss. She didn't notice that assembly had ended and the girls were all filing out. Before she could leave, Dr. Hanover called to her from the stage.

"Mary Margaret. Can you come up here and meet Mrs. Abbott, please?"

Her feet felt like lead as she climbed the stairs to the stage and walked over towards the podium where the two women were standing, visiting with a few other faculty members.

"Oh, good. Mrs. Abbott, I wanted you to meet Mary Margaret Richardson. She is the sponsor of the Social Justice Club here at Hutchison. Mary Margaret, this is Elizabeth Abbott."

Mary Margaret shook hands with Elizabeth. Somehow she managed to say, "Thank you for a wonderful talk. We are so glad to have you here today." She couldn't take her eyes off Elizabeth. She was one of the most beautiful women she had ever seen—Black or White. Her large brown eyes and elegant high cheekbones were set off by an abundance of curly hair in the latest Afro style. Her tiny waist and hips curved gracefully into her long legs, set off by stylish heels. But her engaging smile was her best feature.

Mary Margaret had seen John's picture in the paper once or twice, and she knew that he was involved with civil rights law. But the fact that they had both been in Memphis all these years really hit home when she met his wife. And heard about his children.

Dr. Hanover interrupted her thoughts. "Mary Margaret went to school at Ole Miss."

"Oh, really? What years were you there?" Elizabeth asked.

"I was there from 1966-1970."

"Oh, that's the same years as John."

"Yes—yes, I know. I mean, we met in an English class our freshman year. He was the smartest kid in the class."

"That doesn't surprise me. Were you also active in the racial demonstrations?"

"No. I'm kind of ashamed to say that I was pretty much cloistered away at the sorority house when I wasn't at parties. I wasn't brave enough to be involved in any protests, and I regret that now."

"But look at the great work you're doing with the Social Justice Club here."

"Oh, I'm not really doing much. The girls are amazing. They are so open to the changes that need to happen where civil rights are concerned. I know we've come a long way since the '60s, but we've still got a long way to go."

After meeting Elizabeth, Mary Margaret found herself drawn to the library to search for articles about John on microfilm. The internet was new in 1993, so lots of information wasn't yet available on the web. She was hungry to read about John's career and to picture what his life had been like. She printed off several articles and took them home to read later.

When Walker arrived home from work, he saw the articles on top of Mary Margaret's classroom materials on the table in the kitchen. "What's all this about some Black judge and the NAACP?"

"Oh, that? I was doing some research for my Social Justice Club on the civil rights movement in Memphis, and I ran across those."

Walker picked up the top page—a newspaper article from 1974 about desegregation in the Memphis school system and the NAACP Legal Defense Fund. John's name was included with others at the law firm where he worked. Walker thumbed through several pages and came to an older piece about the protest at Ole Miss in 1970, and again saw John's name.

"Hey, isn't this guy one of the people who got arrested our senior year for protesting during that concert at Fulton Chapel?"

"Yes, I think so." Mary Margaret kept her tone casual.

"And now he's a judge and major civil rights attorney here, right?"

"Right again. Turns out his wife works at Porter-Leath, and she was the guest speaker at assembly at Hutchison today. They have two boys who go to MUS. Small world, huh?"

Walker nodded and put the paper back down on the table. "What's for dinner? I'm famished." He looked a little weary.

"It will take about an hour. Would you like a drink and maybe an appetizer?" Mary Margaret pulled a casserole from the refrigerator and turned the oven on.

"I could use a Jack Daniels and maybe a handful of peanuts."

"Whiskey on a weeknight? Hard day at work?"

Walker didn't talk to Mary Margaret about work very often. But since taking over the business after his father's retirement the previous year, the pressure had been building.

"I shouldn't complain. Business is booming. Everything has come back stronger than ever after that recession a couple of years ago. But growth comes with growing pains. I guess that's what I'm feeling."

Mary Margaret poured Walker's whiskey over ice and made herself a vodka martini. "Let's sit in the living room while the casserole heats up."

Relaxing back into his leather chair and propping his feet up on the matching ottoman, Walker sipped his whiskey and smiled at his wife. "If you had asked me when we first got married and I went to work with my father whether I thought Richardson Properties would be where it is today, I'm not sure I would have thought so."

"How do you mean?" Mary Margaret asked.

"Well, when I started here in 1970, we mainly did sales and leasing of retail properties. Then we expanded to developing mixed-use projects."

"I know all that, Walker. I've been right here with you all these years." Mary Margaret sipped her martini and leaned forward from her chair towards Walker. "The business is doing okay, right?"

"Oh, yes. But some of the younger guys I brought on board after Dad left have come to me with ideas for expanding into the self-storage business."

"That's a different direction altogether, right?"

"It is, and it would require different creative energies and management skills on the part of my people. But it's the wave of the future. The group that started Storage City is making a killing."

"I guess the question is, do you want to expand into that business," Mary Margaret said. "Or do you need to?"

"It looks like a win-win, so long as the managers I've brought on board are excited about it. But I have to admit it's been keeping me up at night."

"The girls and I are just happy that you're home most evenings and weekends. I'm really glad you didn't pursue that development in Nashville."

"Me, too." Walker smiled and finished his bourbon. "*Mmmm* . . . something smells delicious!"

"Oh goodness! I almost forgot the chicken casserole!" She turned and called out, "Girls! Dinner!"

Emily and Claire came running downstairs at the same time, Claire laughing and Emily pouting. Both were bursting with energy, and for Emily, at thirteen, hormones.

"Mom! Make Claire leave me alone!" Emily whined.

"She's two years younger than you, and yet you always let her get to you," Walker said, following them into the kitchen.

"That's because she's such a baby," Emily said.

"What did she do this time?" Mary Margaret asked.

"She keeps saying I'm in love with Michael Callahan, but we're just friends."

"Okay, help me get supper on the table and we'll sort this out."

Mary Margaret's chicken casserole was a favorite with the whole family. It was her mother's recipe, and it had been published in the 1978 edition of *Southern Sideboards*—the famous cookbook put out every year by the Junior League of Jackson.

"Who is this Michael Callahan?" Walker asked.

"He's a ninth grader at MUS!" Claire said. "And he and Emily are on the phone all the time. And Saturday when we went to the library he was there, and they sat at a table alone for two hours."

"At the library?" Mary Margaret looked at Walker and grinned. "My, that sounds serious."

"We were just studying and talking about books and stories and stuff," Emily said.

"Yeah, sure!" Claire said.

"Now wait a minute, Claire," Mary Margaret said. "They could really be discussing literature. Who are your favorite writers, Emily?"

"Oh, I like everything by Eudora Welty, and I loved *The Heart is a Lonely Hunter* by Carson McCullers."

"Isn't that a little old for her?" Walker asked Mary Margaret.

"Not at Hutchison. And definitely not for Emily. She's been reading a couple of grades above her level for years, right Emily?" She gave Emily a proud smile.

"I guess so, but I haven't really thought about it. I just know I love reading more than anything else. And so does Michael."

"What does he like to read?"

"He loves anything historical. He recently read a book called *The Confessions of Nat Turner.* He was telling me all about it at the library on Saturday."

"Isn't that about the Negro slave who led that big revolt, back in the early 1800s?" Walker asked. "Kind of heavy reading for a—how old is Matthew?"

"He's fifteen, Dad, but he's really smart."

"Why the interest in slavery?"

Before Emily could answer, Claire blurted out, "Probably because he's Black."

"And he goes to MUS?" Walker asked. "I didn't realize MUS had African American students."

Finishing up her second helping of chicken casserole, Emily said, "Yes. We met at the middle school mixer last year, and then we've run into each other at the library a few times. It's no big deal." She put down her fork and stood to leave the table. "I've got a French test tomorrow. May I be excused?"

"Sure, that's fine, sweetheart," Walker said, smiling at Mary Margaret.

"Oh, sure, she's got a test, so I get stuck with the dishes, right?" It was Claire's turn to pout.

"It's my fault that supper was so late tonight, so you can head on upstairs with your sister," Mary Margaret said.

"Delicious meal, darling," Walker said, carrying his plate to the sink. "Need some help here?"

"No, thanks. You've had a rough day. And truth is, I don't mind a little quiet time in the kitchen alone."

As soon as Walker and the girls left the kitchen, Mary Margaret's mind was anything but quiet. Rinsing the dishes and loading the dishwasher, all she could think about was Emily and this Black boy discussing literature at the library. She had been only five years older than Emily when she and John Abbott were studying in the library together at Ole Miss back in 1966. That felt like a lifetime ago, and in many ways, it was. *Will things be different for my girls when they go to college? Will their choices about relationships and race be easier?*

The next decade held some of the answers, as Emily went off to Ole Miss to study literature and creative writing in 1998. The racial atmosphere had improved on the campus. In 2000, the student body elected their first Black president, a political science major. That year Blacks made up twelve percent of the university's 10,000 students. A second Black student body president was elected the following year. The 2002–2003 academic year was dedicated to the 40th anniversary of the integration of the university.

In remembrance of the events of 1963—including the enrollment of James Meredith as the first Black student at Ole Miss— the university planned numerous discussions and events, calling the commemoration "Open Doors: 40 years of Opportunity." Emily graduated in 2002 but stayed at the university to get her MFA in creative writing, which she finished in 2004. Her thesis—a study of race relations in Mississippi—was later published and she was invited to teach at Ole Miss the following year. She stayed on, teaching and working on short stories and novels.

Claire stayed in Memphis, studying theater and dance at the University of Memphis and becoming active in local theater. In 2004 she followed her dreams to New York, where she continued to study acting while auditioning for parts on Broadway.

Mary Margaret loved theater, and she and Walker had season tickets to the Memphis Symphony Orchestra and the Orpheum Theater, which were both downtown. After enjoying many performances at both venues over the years, Mary Margaret approached Walker about an idea she had been mulling over in her mind. It was 2009, and *The Color Purple* was playing at The Orpheum. Their tickets were for the Saturday afternoon matinee.

"Hey, Walker, how would you like to get away somewhere pretty and relaxing this weekend, without having to drive more than thirty minutes?"

"Is this a trick question? And I thought we had tickets for a play at The Orpheum this weekend."

"No. And yes." Mary Margaret laughed. "I mean no, it's not a trick question, and yes we do have tickets for The Orpheum. So, I thought maybe we could spend the weekend in that boutique hotel on Mud Island, you know, the one right at the entrance to Harbor Town? We could get a room with a view of the Mississippi River, sleep in both mornings, and enjoy dinner at the restaurant downstairs from our room. There's also a great coffee shop just down the street, and a casual bar and grill next door. How does that sound?"

"That sounds like you've been planning this for a while," Walker smiled. "But it actually sounds like a good idea. Have you already booked our room?"

"Oh, you know me well, don't you? It's a suite. And the hotel is only about five minutes from The Orpheum. We could drive or take a cab."

The weekend was everything Mary Margaret had envisioned, and more. After checking out of the hotel on Sunday afternoon, they drove north on Island Drive to explore the "island"—which was really a peninsula—a bit more. Lots of people were walking, jogging, and riding bikes along the river. Near the end of the waterfront, just as the road took a ninety-degree right turn, back towards the city, Mary Margaret noticed a large building facing the river. The sign out front said, "Sunset Park Senior Living."

"Huh. I didn't know there was a senior living facility down here, did you?" Mary Margaret asked Walker, who glanced out the window as he continued to drive.

"Yes, I heard they were building one. Didn't know it was finished. Does it look nice?"

"I couldn't get a good look, but wow, what a location! Right here on the river. I guess it's good to know about it in case either of us needs a place like this one day."

That day came sooner than they had expected, as Walker began to show symptoms of cognitive decline—both at work and at home.

"Where's the—what do you call that thing?" He said to Margaret one Saturday, walking around the den, looking under a stack of newspapers and behind the cushion in his recliner.

"What thing, dear?"

"You know, the little thing that you use to turn the TV on and change the channels."

Mary Margaret looked up from the book she was reading. "You mean the remote? It's over there on the coffee table."

"Damn it," Walker said, picking up the remote and pointing it at the television.

"Why are you so upset? It wasn't even lost."

"It's not that I couldn't find the remote . . . it's that I couldn't remember what it's called. Happens all the time lately. The other day at work I couldn't remember what to call a calculator."

"Oh, honey, that happens to all of us. I wouldn't worry about it."

As the months and years went by, Walker's memory loss became more obvious. He began to forget how to do simple tasks, like making coffee or using his electric shaver. He and Mary Margaret would be having a conversation and he would just stop in the middle of a sentence, searching in vain for the words.

Finally, in 2010, he sold the business to two of his younger managers, and he and Mary Margaret made a move that surprised their daughters. They bought one of those stately homes right on the river in Harbor town. Ever the cautious older daughter, Emily was the first to express her concerns.

"What are you thinking, Mom?" she asked on a weekend visit from Oxford. "Don't most people scale down when they retire? And all your friends are out east. You will be a half hour from most of the people you know."

"Let's go for a drive," Mary Margaret said. "I want to show you something."

As they drove from Mary Margaret and Walker's home in East Memphis, through Midtown, and finally over the bridge onto Mud Island, Mary Margaret reminded her daughter of all the things she and Walker enjoyed downtown—the symphony, The Orpheum Theater, and so many nice restaurants. And then she turned onto Island Drive.

"Okay, I know it's beautiful here," Emily said. "And yes, these houses are amazing."

She turned into the first entrance to the neighborhood and pointed out the restaurants, coffee shop, boutique grocery store, twenty-four-hour fitness center, dry cleaners, and nail salon all on one block.

"We can walk to these places, or ride a golf cart." She laughed as a woman parked her golf cart in front of the fitness center and hopped out with her yoga mat in one hand and a water bottle in the other.

As they continued through the neighborhood with its winding

streets, sidewalks, and numerous parks and duck ponds, Emily began to see what drew her mother to the place. But then Mary Margaret turned back out onto Island Drive and continued north, past the neighborhood and a couple of apartment complexes, until they arrived at Sunset Park. She pulled into the drive and stopped in front of the main building.

Emily looked at the sign and then at her mother. "So, what's this? You and dad are only in your sixties. Are ya'll moving into a senior living facility?"

"No. But I want to be close to one for when—for when I can't take care of your father at home. This would be just down the street from our house."

Emily's eyes filled with tears. "Oh, Mom, I didn't realize it was getting that bad. I can totally see why this is a good idea. And you're still just over an hour from my place in Oxford."

They joined a bridge club, and even took up golf. Their friends in the bridge club were the first to comment on Walker's decline.

"It's not that he can't remember which cards have been played," one of them said after an evening of cards. "It's that he doesn't even remember how the game is played."

And that was the end of that social outlet.

Golf lasted a bit longer, as Walker's muscle memory kicked in when he picked up a club and swung at the ball. But Mary Margaret found herself telling him which club to use for each shot, when it had always been the other way around. A diagnosis of Alzheimer's confirmed their suspicions, and their sunset years were more like one long, slow, climb backwards down a steep cliff.

As Walker's cognitive abilities declined, he also became frustrated and sometimes belligerent towards Mary Margaret. Embarrassed by his incontinence and angry about his loss of control—both mentally and physically—he lashed out at the people she hired to help with his care, and often at Mary Margaret herself. Returning from her writing group meeting one day several years into his decline, she found him screaming at the aide who was trying to help him back into his bed for a nap.

"Walker!" Mary Margaret hurried into the room. "Robert is just trying to help you."

"Robert?" Walker's face showed confusion and fear. "Who the hell is Robert?"

"It's me, Mr. Richardson," Robert said, "I've been taking care of you today, and lots of days before this."

"Have you given him a sedative?" Mary Margaret asked.

"No, ma'am. He wouldn't take it. Pushed it out of my hand and threw the glass of water across the room."

Mary Margaret looked at the broken glass on the floor near the window, and back at Walker, who was still sitting up on the edge of the bed. "Honey, let's lie down for a little rest now, okay? I'll get you a nice glass of juice and something to help you feel better."

She was able to get Walker to take the sedative, and when he finally went to sleep, she fell apart at the kitchen table. Robert joined her, bringing them both a cup of coffee.

"How long have you been taking care of Alzheimer's patients, Robert?" Mary Margaret asked.

"Long time, Mrs. Richardson. Probably twenty years or more."

"So, you've seen this before, these outbursts?"

"Sure, plenty of times. It just comes with the disease. He doesn't mean anything by it."

"Oh, I know that. It's not that I'm taking it personally. It's just that—well, I wonder how long I can handle having him here." Tears filled her eyes. "Do you think it's time for me to put him in a facility?"

"That's a decision for you and your doctor to make, ma'am. Some people can keep their loved ones at home 'til the end, but some just need more help. And sometimes it's actually a blessing for people in Mr. Richardson's condition to be in a place where he's safe and all his needs are met."

"You sound like you're speaking from experience, Robert."

"Yes, ma'am. I worked at a couple of those places for years before doing in-home care. You know, one of the best places for that happens to be right down the road from your house. Have you seen Sunset Park? You could visit and see what you think."

Sunset Park's long-term care center turned out to be a godsend for Walker, and for Mary Margaret. At first she felt guilty for putting him there—that was in 2012—but as time went by and cruelly erased his memory of her, she noticed that he seemed happy in his new world. He was always smiling when she visited, especially when his favorite aide would walk into the room.

"Oh, Mr. Walker, look who's here to see you today! Your beautiful bride!"

His eyes would light up, but Margaret could tell that he was responding more to the presence of the aide than to her. At first that hurt her feelings, and she had to keep reminding herself that it was the disease that caused Walker to forget her. She could only handle spending an hour or two with him each day, and the social worker at the home even said that was the recommended amount of time for visits with Alzheimer's patients. She didn't know whether she said that because it was true or just to make Mary Margaret feel better, but somehow it freed her to spend more time doing things in the community. In addition to the writing group she had joined, she found a women's bridge club and a book club. And a wonderful yoga class for seniors.

The hardest times were the evenings, alone in their home. She had just read *The Hours* by Michael Cunningham, and often found herself bemoaning the hours before her, as she wondered how much longer Walker would live and what she might do with the rest of her years. She had been keeping a journal since the beginning of her husband's illness, and she began writing a memoir. As she shared chapters of it with her writing group, they encouraged her to keep going, and to consider publishing it one day. *Maybe,* she thought. *After Walker's gone.*

People can't, unhappily, invent their mooring posts, their lovers and their friends, any more than they can invent their parents. Life gives these and also takes them away, *and the great difficulty is to say 'Yes' to life.*

—James Baldwin

CHAPTER 9

John and Elizabeth (1970-2015)

After graduating from college, John Abbott spent the next three years in law school. Those years in Oxford were not without more racial unrest, and the BSU became more active than ever. They wrote a new constitution and bylaws, organized a book-exchange program, and set up a student emergency loan fund. The president of the organization was quoted in *The Daily Mississippian* saying, "I plan to establish Black awareness and concerns to unify and maintain Black power and identity. The Black Student Union will engage in the destruction of any racist or fascist system which may try to oppress, harass, or intimidate Black people."

While John agreed with these goals, he also knew that he needed to keep a low profile so that he could finish law school.

One morning during his second year he was studying in the library when a cute young woman sat across from him at one of the long tables. John did a double take when he saw how much she looked like Marsha Hunt, the actress from the rock musical *Hair*. She was even prettier, if that was possible. Thick black lashes set off her dark brown eyes. Her oval-shaped face was surrounded by a perfectly coiffed Afro. Large, yellow ceramic hoops with tiny blue flowers painted on them hung from her earlobes.

John studied quietly for an hour or more—or more like he tried to study—and caught her looking at him more than once. When she started packing up her books to leave, he did the same and they walked to the door of the library together. He held the door open, and when they stepped outside, she made the first move.

"Hi. I'm Elizabeth Tate." Her smile almost melted his heart instantly.

"I'm John Abbott. Want to grab a cup of coffee at the Union?"

"I've got a better idea. My house is just five minutes from campus. And my car is in the parking lot behind the library."

"Your house?" John blushed and looked away.

Elizabeth laughed. "I just meant I've got better coffee—even an espresso maker."

John looked at his watch. It was ten and his next class was at noon. It was risky, but man was she beautiful. They walked to her car—a bright yellow Volkswagen Beetle—and John opened the driver's door for Elizabeth. He had to duck to get in on the passenger's side. His knees were crammed until he slid the seat back.

"Your last passenger must have been a midget!"

It was the second time he had heard Elizabeth's delicious laugh in the past ten minutes.

She skillfully maneuvered the car out of the parking space she had creatively invented in the far corner of the lot, wielding the four-speed manual gear stick like it was an extension of her right arm. As they were exiting, a White security guard pulled in. She flashed her winning smile and waved at the officer as she passed him.

"Hi, Rick! Beautiful day, huh?"

To John's surprise the officer waved back and hollered, "Hi, Lizzie. Sure is. Be careful out there."

"Um, how do you know that guy?" John asked.

"Rick? Oh, we go way back."

John decided not to inquire about Rick. Instead, he patted the dashboard of the car and asked, "What year is this, by the way?"

"It's a 1967. My old man got it for me when I graduated from high school."

"That was nice. Where was high school?"

"It was actually here. In Oxford." She looked at John for a second just as they left the campus and headed down a shady street. "That's how I know Rick, by the way. He worked in town when I was a kid. At a car dealership. He was a salesman, and my dad was a mechanic."

"So, why is Rick working for campus security now?"

"He said he was getting too old for the pressure of selling cars, so he retired early and went to work for the university."

"What about your dad?"

"He's still working on cars. Doesn't see any way to do something better, since he never went to college. Wants to be sure I get a good education."

They stopped in front of a white clapboard house with a green roof and shingles. "Well, here we are. Ready for some coffee?"

"Sure." John followed her inside. The house was furnished with simple but tasteful pieces, a few antiques, and family pictures on the walls. John noticed one in the dining room—Elizabeth as a young girl with people who must have been her parents.

"Nice house."

"Thanks. It's my dad's. Come on in the kitchen. Do you like espresso?"

"Sounds great." He sat at her kitchen table and watched her work her magic with an Italian espresso pot.

"I can steam some milk if you want a cappuccino."

"Even better. So, what were you pretending to study back there at the library?"

She smiled at him over her shoulder as she continued working on their drinks. "Human behavior and the social environment."

John gave her a questioning look. "I've never heard of that class.

What year are you?"

"I'm a first-year graduate student. Working on my MSW—Master of Social Work."

"Oh, that's why I've never heard of it. So where did you do your undergrad?"

"I went to Jackson State. Graduated in 1971. You?"

"I went to Ole Miss. Graduated in 1970. But wait, you were at Jackson State when those students were killed in '70? Were you on campus when it happened?"

Elizabeth brought their cappuccinos to the table, sat, and took a deep breath. "Oh, I was there all right. I was inside my dorm—Alexander Hall—when I heard a lot of noise outside my window. I looked out and there were a bunch of kids screaming. I couldn't tell why at first, but later I heard that a truck was on fire on Lynch Street—a street we had to cross to get to class—and the police and fire department had just arrived on the scene. Evidently the police, about seventy-five of them in full riot gear, heard a bottle being dropped and thought it was a sniper on top of my dorm, so they opened fire. Within thirty seconds they killed two students and wounded twelve."

"Were you hurt?" John leaned forward against the table.

"Not me. Lots of students were hurt by flying glass and debris from the windows in the dorm. I was lucky. One of the students who was killed, Phillip Gibbs, was a junior studying political science. He was also married with an eighteen-month-old son, and his wife was pregnant with another baby."

"I heard about the shootings," John said, "but I didn't know the details. What were the riots about?"

"Lots of people think the students were rioting about the Vietnam war, like they were at Kent State. But it wasn't about that at all. It was really about students being yelled at, and things being thrown at them by White drivers as they crossed Lynch Street, which goes through the middle of campus. The drivers acted like they were trying to run the students over. So the students protested to have the street end before it got to the campus, so they wouldn't have to be harassed on their way to class every day."

"What was the deal about a fire?" John asked.

"So, some people who lived in the surrounding neighborhood pulled a dump truck into the middle of Lynch Street and set it on fire to literally stop the traffic from going through campus."

"Didn't you say two students were killed? Who was the other one?"

"His name was James Green, but he wasn't a student at Jackson State. He was actually a senior and track star at Jim Hill High School. He was walking home from working at a grocery store. When he was across the street from Alexander Hall, the police started to fire. They shot and killed him."

"So, he wasn't even involved in the riot at all?"

"No. He wasn't anywhere near it. They literally had to turn around and fire in the complete opposite direction to kill him. Green had a track scholarship to UCLA in the fall and was going to compete in Olympic trials."

"Oh, man. That's even worse than I had heard."

"So, what about the protests at Ole Miss? Were you involved in any of that?"

John nodded but looked at his watch. "I'll have to tell you about it another time. I need to get to class now. Can you give me a ride back to campus?"

"Sure. If you'll promise to come back another time. I'd love for you to meet my father."

"Now that's not something a girl usually says to a guy she's just met." They both laughed as they headed out to Elizabeth's car.

Wooing Elizabeth was such a different experience than his attempts with Mary Margaret. Of course they met with no objections from Whites on campus, and if their presence brought any stares as they spent time together at the Grove or in the library, it was only because they were such a great-looking couple.

By the end of John's second year of law school, which was Elizabeth's first of two years of graduate school, they were ready to move their relationship to the next stage. John had come to really like Elizabeth's father, and they spent lots of time together at the home he shared with his daughter. He learned that Elizabeth's mother had died from cancer when her daughter was twelve—about the age she was in the family photograph John had seen in their house the first day he visited. One day, John paid her father a visit at the car dealership. They found him in the service department working on a radiator.

"Hello, Mr. Tate," John said, stepping around the various tools and automobile parts that were strewn around on the dirty concrete floor.

Mr. Tate looked up from under the hood of the car with an expression of surprise.

"John. I wasn't expecting to see you here. Your car need some work done?"

"No sir. I just need a moment to speak with you privately—without Elizabeth around."

Mr. Tate looked up from the car hood. "Well, let's step inside where it's air conditioned. Let me wash some of this grease off my hands first." He turned to a sink on the wall in the shop, scrubbed his hands, and then pointed to a door that led inside the building.

Once inside, they moved into a small employee lounge. "Want a cold Coke?" Mr. Tate motioned to the drink machine.

"Yes, I think I would," John said, his voice sounding a bit gravelly.

"You got a cold?" Mr. Tate asked as he pulled two Cokes from the machine and motioned to an empty table with two chairs.

"Oh, no. I guess—I guess I'm just a little nervous is all." They sat in two old chrome chairs with faded red plastic seat covers. John set his Coke down on the table and placed his hands in his lap.

"You see, sir, Elizabeth and I have been dating for a while now, and we really care about each other."

"I'm sure you do, or you wouldn't still be spending so much time together." Mr. Tate took a drink of his Coke and smiled, looking straight into John's face. "And I have to say, I haven't seen Lizzy this happy in a long time. Maybe ever."

"I'm glad to hear that. You see, the reason I'm here is, I'd like to discuss our future—mine and Elizabeth's."

"I'm listening." Mr. Tate's smile grew, and he seemed to be enjoying John's nervousness.

"Well, okay, here it is then. Do I have your permission to marry Elizabeth?" A wave of nausea hit just as he got the words out, but quickly subsided with Mr. Tate's answer.

"I say it's about time, John. And yes, you have my permission and—although you didn't exactly ask for it—my blessing!"

Both men stood and John offered his hand across the table. Mr. Tate grabbed it with a firm hold, and then stepped around the table and pulled John into an embrace, slapping him on the back and laughing. When they pulled away, Mr. Tate kept his hands on John's shoulders and his eyes filled with tears. "I only wish Elizabeth's mother was here to see this day."

"I do, too, sir." The gravelly sound in John's throat was gone. For now. Next, he would have to propose to Elizabeth. And he didn't have money for a ring. As if reading his thoughts, Mr. Tate said, "John, I was about to call it quits for the day. Why don't you come down to the house with me. I need to show you something."

John drove to the house, pulled up in front, and followed Mr. Tate inside.

"Wait right here." Mr. Tate indicated a chair in the living room and disappeared to the back of the house. He returned holding a small, worn leather box. He opened the box to reveal a velvet lining, also worn. In the middle was a ring with a small diamond. He pulled the ring out of the box and handed it to John, who stared at it in his open palm.

"This was Elizabeth's mother's. I gave it to her when I asked her to marry me. It had been my grandmother's, so it's been in the family for three—now four—generations. I'd be mighty proud if you'd give it to Elizabeth."

John was speechless. He really had wondered how he would afford an engagement ring, and he didn't want to borrow more money, since he already had law school loans. He turned the ring over in his hand, holding it up between his thumb and index finger and looking at it in the light coming in the front window. The diamond was small, but the cut was lovely. The white gold band was in excellent condition. Mrs. Tate had only worn it for thirteen years before she died. Before he had a chance to respond, he heard the kitchen door open and Elizabeth's voice calling, "Hey, Daddy!" And then, "Is that John's car out front?"

John slipped the ring into his pocket quickly as she came into the living room from the kitchen. Mr. Tate seemed unaware that he was still holding the jewelry box, until Elizabeth walked over to him and said, "What's in the box, Daddy?"

Mr. Tate looked at the box in his hand, and then at John, before answering, "Oh, nothing, honey."

Elizabeth gave them each a hug.

"So, is someone going to tell me what's going on here?" She looked at John and added, "And what are you doing here? I thought you knew I had a seminar this afternoon."

John looked at Mr. Tate, who nodded, and they both smiled. John turned to Elizabeth, and got down on one knee in front of her. Before she could ask more questions, he said, "Elizabeth Tate, will you do me the honor of becoming my wife?" He reached into his pocket and pulled out the ring, and reached for her left hand. Holding the ring near her hand, he looked into her eyes and waited for her answer.

"Oh, my goodness! Yes! Of course!" she almost screamed, and John placed the ring on her finger. A perfect fit. She looked at the ring and then threw her arms around John and kissed him on the mouth, hardly remembering that her father was there.

"Ahem," Mr. Tate let out a fake cough to get her attention.

Looking at her father she said, "Wait, did you know about this?"

Her father nodded, his smile now accompanied by tears. "John came by the shop to ask my permission. Then I brought him here to—well, to give him my blessing and a gift."

"A gift? What gift?"

"It's on your finger, honey. That was your mother's engagement ring."

Elizabeth burst into tears and fell into her father's arms. John couldn't remember when he had been happier. Well, maybe once, with Mary Margaret, but that happiness was part of a life that wasn't going to be his. The one right in front of him had promise.

John had taken Elizabeth to Memphis to meet his family a few months earlier, but their next trip brought more tears of joy as they shared their news with his parents. His mother and Elizabeth spent what seemed like hours together poring over patterns for wedding gowns and shopping for fabrics. John knew that Elizabeth wished her own mother could be there for these preparations, but he was glad to see her bonding with his mother.

They were married at the end of the summer in a small wedding at Burns United Methodist Church, the first African American Church built in Oxford. John was interested to learn that Harrison Stearns, a slave of William Stearns—the first dean of the law school at Ole Miss—initiated the building of the church in 1865. William Stearns died in 1867, before the property deed could be finished, but his wife, Mary Stearns, completed the deal with Harrison in 1868. It was known as The Colored Church at Oxford. It was somehow comforting to John to know that Dean Stearns had been a part of that historic building, although he hoped that one day his family would worship side by side with White believers.

The couple moved in with her father for their last year at Ole Miss, to save money on rent, and so that Mr. Tate and Elizabeth could have more time together. John and Elizabeth planned to move to Memphis after graduation, and they both knew the separation would be hard on her father.

"You could come with us, you know," Elizabeth said as she was packing up her things at the house one day.

"And do what? I've still got fifteen years 'til I retire from the shop, and who knows what kind of work I could get in Memphis. Besides, the house here is paid for and I'm not ready for big city life."

Elizabeth wasn't sure if she was ready for the big city either. She would find out soon, as she and John moved into a carriage house behind a beautiful Georgian revival home in the elite South Parkway-Heiskell Farm District of south Memphis. The neighborhood, which included a self-contained, three-block segment of the Memphis Parkway System, was made up of twenty-seven original houses built in the early 1900s. It was home to well-to-do Black families, like John and Elizabeth's landlord, who was one of the founders of the first integrated law firm in Memphis.

Upon graduation, John had been offered an entry-level job at the firm, and when his boss had asked where the newlyweds planned to live, John had said they didn't know. So his boss invited them to rent the carriage house behind his home on South Parkway.

John found kindred spirits among the firm's young, aggressive, idealistic, hip litigators who believed they could change the world. A colleague who had graduated from Vanderbilt Law School had played football against John at a rival school when they were both in high school. For both men, it was rewarding to now be playing for the same side as adults, back in their hometown. Working at the firm set a path for John to be an advocate for the disenfranchised against powerful interests. The firm handled the Memphis city school desegregation case and many of the civil rights cases in the city.

John worked endless overtime hours during his first three years—he'd taken a side job as a referee at juvenile court to pay off his law school loans. He continued to pay his dues, working tirelessly to get NAACP Memphis Branch members out of jail.

He and Elizabeth were looking forward to buying a house of

their own, hopefully in the South Parkway neighborhood where they had been renting their little carriage house. Their dream came true in 1976, when John became the youngest and first Black judge appointed to General Sessions Court. Elizabeth was ecstatic over the 1920s Beaux Arts home they were able to purchase, and she and John began planning to have a family.

She hadn't been in a hurry to have children when they first married. She was anxious to put her graduate degree to use, and was happy to land a job at Porter-Leath Children's Center. Porter-Leath was founded in 1951 as an asylum for orphans. Over the years it added comprehensive child welfare services for children and their families. By the time Elizabeth joined the Center, it was the best facility in Memphis providing treatment for children with emotional problems, as well as dependent and neglected children. She fell in love with many of the children she helped there, and by the end of the 1970s Elizabeth had given birth to two boys.

John's father died in 1977, and his mother moved in with them the same year. She retired from her years as a seamstress and stepped into the role of nanny to her two grandsons while Elizabeth continued her work at Porter-Leath.

The 1980s brought decisions about school for their boys. The public elementary school they were zoned for—like many traditionally Black schools—hadn't changed much with mandatory desegregation. Most of the White kids zoned for the school went to private schools instead. Elizabeth and John both wanted a more diverse experience for their boys, and better teachers.

One evening after the boys were asleep, Elizabeth asked John, "What was it like for you, going to a Black neighborhood school in Memphis?"

"It was okay. I really didn't have anything to compare it to. It's where all my friends went."

"I get that, but what about the academic level of the teaching? And the achievements of the students?"

"The percentage that went to college was pretty low. And I caught flack for making good grades."

"I know your law firm worked hard to try to make desegregation work here in Memphis, but it seems like busing and 'white flight' only hurt the schools in the end. And the communities, too, for that matter."

John was quiet as he considered Elizabeth's words. After a while he asked, "What are you getting at?"

Elizabeth took a deep breath. "I was reading about the school at Second Presbyterian Church, you know, the big church on Poplar?"

"Sure, Presbyterian Day School. I know some lawyers whose sons go there. But PDS is segregated, isn't it?"

"Well, of course it's predominantly White, but there are a few Black students there. And it wasn't formed as a segregationist school. It started in 1949, and initially it went up through grade nine. But in 1955 the school shifted grades seven through nine over to MUS, which is where most of the boys from PDS go for upper school."

John had been reading when Elizabeth started speaking, but now he put down his book and looked directly at her as she mentioned Memphis University School. "You're serious about this, aren't you?"

"Yes, and I think you should be, too. MUS has been around since 1893. Their mission statement says they prepare the boys for competitive colleges. Isn't that what we both want for our sons?"

"Of course it is, but, how would it look for a Black civil rights lawyer and judge to send his boys to a private White school?"

"And when have you ever cared what other people thought about you?"

By the mid-1980s both boys were enrolled at PDS and seemed to thrive there. They each moved seamlessly from PDS to MUS when they finished sixth grade.

Elizabeth continued her work at Porter-Leath. In 1993 she became involved with Sarah's Place, an emergency care facility for neglected or abused children, which had just opened on the Porter-

Leath campus. Shortly after beginning her new position, she received a phone call from the headmistress at Hutchison, the private girls' school next door to MUS. She invited Elizabeth to speak at the Hutchison upper school's assembly.

Elizabeth was impressed that Hutchison, like MUS, had a smattering of Black students. She was more impressed with their Social Justice Club, and the club's sponsor, Mary Margaret Richardson. That evening after her talk, she told John and the boys about the event at supper.

"The girls at Hutchison have a Social Justice Club, and several of them asked very informed questions after my talk."

John answered, "Uh huh" with a mouth full of ribs. He had picked up the barbeque at Cozy Corner on his way home from work. He not only believed they had the best pork ribs in Memphis—which was saying a lot—but he also loved that they were owned by a Black family.

"I'm sure you did a great job," he added.

"One of the girls asked me if I had a son at MUS," Elizabeth continued. Their oldest son, Martin, perked up at the question.

"What was her name?" he asked.

"She didn't say. But she did say she met you at a party."

Martin's younger brother, James, poked him in the arm with his elbow, both hands still holding onto a half-eaten rib. "Dude! You got a sweetie over at Hutchison?" He was grinning, barbeque sauce dripping from the corners of his mouth.

"Shut up, Jimmy. You're just jealous." Martin couldn't contain his teasing grin.

Elizabeth and John exchanged a smile, expressive of the joy they both received from their boys.

"After my talk, the headmistress introduced me to the woman who sponsors the Social Justice Club. She also teaches English and literature at Hutchison. Evidently, she was at Ole Miss the same time you were there as an undergrad, John."

"Really. What a coincidence."

"Yes, and she said she knew you. Evidently y'all were in freshman English together. She said you were the smartest in the class."

John put down the rib he was holding and wiped his mouth on his napkin. Looking at Elizabeth, he asked, "What was her name?"

"Mrs. Richardson, I think."

"No, I mean her first name."

"Oh, I think it was Mary Margaret. Beautiful White woman. And so enthusiastic about civil rights."

John's heart raced at hearing Mary Margaret's name. He tried to keep a neutral expression, taking a long drink of his beer before speaking again. He remembered that she was going to be teaching at Hutchison when she graduated from Ole Miss in 1970. But he had tried not to think about her during all the years he and Elizabeth had been married. And he had been successful, most of the time, except when he would hear one of the jazz numbers he and Mary Margaret had danced to on that fateful night their freshman year. Then he had to keep himself from going there—back to the memory of her bouncy blond ponytail and her smile that radiated sunshine. And her lips.

"John?" Elizabeth said. "Are you listening to me?"

"What? Oh, yes, sorry. I was just trying to remember that woman—the girl from Ole Miss. I think we might have studied together for English tests a couple of times."

"You hung out with a White girl?" Martin piped up. "On the Ole Miss campus in the 1960s? That was gutsy."

John immediately wished he hadn't shared the memory. "We did get a few stares from people in the library." He stopped there. He had made it over twenty years without telling Elizabeth about Mary Margaret. No reason to muddy the waters now. They were happy, weren't they?

Yes, they were. John's success as a judge was everything he had hoped to achieve. Two more decades brought the realization of many dreams for their family. The boys both went to good universities. Martin went to law school at Harvard and returned to Memphis to work at the law firm where his father had started. And James ended up teaching political science at Ole Miss. Elizabeth continued her work at Porter-Leath until 2013, when she retired after forty years. John was hoping to continue his work for a few more years, until something happened that changed everything.

"Oh, my," Adele said after listening to John and Mary Margaret's stories of their lives with their families in Memphis. "What amazing journeys you each have had."

As they sipped coffee and ate sandwiches, John and Mary Margaret reflected on what happened as the years went by. Both couples thought they were moving towards their sunset years with their spouses of several decades. But that's when John and Mary Margaret's dreams were replaced with new chapters neither would ever had anticipated.

"How did you two find each other again? I can't wait to hear the rest of the story!" Adele said.

Looking at the clock, Mary Margaret realized that they had been visiting for over two hours. "Maybe it's time for a glass of wine. This might take the rest of the afternoon."

The three of them got up and stretched. Adele walked from the den to the front of the house and looked out the window. A huge barge was headed south on the river, a scene she often saw on her walks. She was a bit envious of Mary Margaret and John's view.

But she wondered what happened to Elizabeth and Walker. She couldn't imagine either couple divorcing after hearing how successful their marriages had turned out. And she still had no idea what any of this had to do with Alzheimer's.

"Oh, there you are," Mary Margaret found Adele gazing out the window in the living room. "Would you prefer to sit in here?"

"That would be lovely. I was just admiring your view."

John found the women in the living room, and he brought with him a tray with three wine glasses and a bottle of Chardonnay. "If this keeps up, we might have to heat up some leftovers for supper!"

"Goodness, am I overstaying my welcome?"

"Of course not," Mary Margaret sat down on the couch next to John, across the coffee table from the chair where Adele was seated. "We've never really told our stories to anyone, well, except for our children, of course."

"I'm curious about how you ended up here, John. It seems, from what you've told me, that Mary Margaret and Walker might have retired here. Is that right?"

Mary Margaret nodded as she took a sip of wine. "And it was lovely . . . for a while." She looked at John with a sad expression, which he returned.

"I guess it's time for the rest of my story with Elizabeth," John said, settling back on the couch and looking wistfully out the window.

After Elizabeth retired from Porter-Leath in 2013, she was restless at home alone. John was still busy with work, and Elizabeth had never had much free time during her career. Working full time for forty years hadn't allowed much time for socializing with friends, and her sons were busy with their own careers.

She volunteered one day a week with the Memphis Child Advocacy Center, which served children who were victims of sexual or physical abuse. Otherwise, she spent a lot of time at home, trying to figure out what to do next. As the months went by, she felt more and more distant from the world around her. Everything began to feel fuzzy.

One day when John came home from work, he found Elizabeth sitting at the kitchen table staring at a cookbook. Pots and pans were strewn around the kitchen, some on the cabinets and others on the floor, along with measuring cups and spoons. A package of frozen chicken breasts was sitting on the counter near the refrigerator, along with a few onions and a bag of potatoes. It was almost 5:30 p.m., and Elizabeth was still in her nightgown and robe, which was uncharacteristic for her. As John walked in the door, she looked up from the table and burst into tears.

John put down his briefcase and moved to the chair beside her, putting his arm around her shoulders. "What's all this?" he asked, looking around at the cluttered kitchen. "Are you writing a cookbook?" His tone was light; hers was not.

"Oh, John, I don't know what's wrong, but I just can't think clearly. I was going to cook some chicken for supper, but—" She covered her face with her hands and wept loudly.

"But, what, dear?" John pulled her into his arms.

Once she caught her breath, she looked at John with fear in her eyes. "Something is wrong with me, John. My brain—it just isn't working right. I can't figure out this simple recipe. And the chicken is hard as a rock."

John looked at the chicken breasts, still in their plastic wrap on the counter. "Well, they're frozen. Does the recipe call for them to be thawed first?"

"I don't know what the damn recipe says, John. I can't . . . I can't read it. The words don't make sense. And when I got the pots and pans out of the cabinet, I dropped some of them on the floor. My hands just wouldn't hold onto them." She held up her hands with the palms towards her face. They were shaking.

Fear gripped John and his mind raced to drastic considerations. Did she have Parkinson's? Was she having a stroke? He rushed to the phone to call their physician. It was after hours and he got the answering service.

"If this is an emergency, please dial 911."

John dialed and explained what was happening.

"If your wife isn't in urgent need of care, I suggest you make an appointment with her physician, but if you don't think it can wait, you should drive her to a nearby emergency room."

He considered what constituted an emergency—chest pain, numbness in her arms, blurry vision, all signs of a stroke or heart attack—but Elizabeth didn't seem to have any of these. He decided to wait and call her physician the next day.

The following months were excruciating, as John took Elizabeth to one doctor after another—including a trip to Mayo Clinic, where she finally received a diagnosis. Elizabeth had Lewy Body Dementia. Some of Elizabeth's symptoms, like muscle problems and tremors, were similar to Parkinson's, which was one reason the disease was often misdiagnosed. She was only sixty-three years old. Unlike Alzheimer's, which more often affects older people, Lewy Body frequently struck younger victims, and the life expectancy was also shorter. The doctors told her she probably wouldn't make it to seventy.

Devastated by the news, John and Elizabeth set out to do everything they could. They traveled to Europe—something Elizabeth had always dreamed about. She needed help with mobility, and eventually even a wheelchair. Back home they made changes to accommodate her diminishing motor skills. John had a hospital bed set up in the sunroom near the kitchen, when Elizabeth could no longer handle the stairs leading up to their bedroom. Eventually John hired home health care aides to be with Elizabeth when he was working. Finally, he retired as a General Sessions Court judge in 2015, but even with him being home full time and with outside help, Elizabeth's care became too much. It was time to consider moving her to a facility, which broke his heart. Elizabeth could barely communicate with words at that point, but her eyes told him she was still there. When he told her about the potential move, she nodded, with tears.

John researched all the long-term care facilities in Memphis, and finally decided on a place on the north end of Mud Island. He could drive there in thirty minutes from their home on South Parkway, and it was close to his son Martin's law office downtown, so Martin would be able to visit easily. His friends wondered why he didn't choose one of the nursing homes in East Memphis, closer to his house. They hadn't seen the view at Sunset Park.

Love does not begin and end the way we seem to think it does.
Love is a battle, love is a war; love is a growing up.

—**James Baldwin,** *Nobody Knows My Name:*
More Notes of a Native Son

CHAPTER 10

Sunset Park (2015)

Martin and James Abbott helped their father with the move. They packed up a few of Elizabeth's favorite things—including the photograph of her as a little girl with her parents, which she had received when her father died a few years earlier. Her study at home was filled with gifts from the families she had helped at Porter-Leath. John placed a worn stuffed bear in her arms after their sons helped her into her wheelchair to transfer her to the car. He tearfully watched as she pulled the bear close in a childlike hug. She still had moments of clarity and seemed to understand that she was leaving her home.

Everyone was quiet on the drive down to Mud Island, Elizabeth sitting on the second seat of Martin's SUV next to John, while Martin drove and James sat with him in front.

"You're still going to be just over an hour from our house in Oxford, Mom," James broke the silence. "We can bring the kids to visit you often. Won't that be great?"

Elizabeth gazed out the window, hugging the bear tightly to her chest, her expression blank.

"And of course and I will just be a few minutes away," Martin offered. Following in his father's footsteps, he had climbed the ladder in the justice system in Memphis and had also become a judge. But his work hadn't left time for a serious relationship, so he was still a bachelor.

After what felt like an eternity, they arrived at Sunset Park around ten that morning. The social worker John had met at the facility had recommended the morning for the move, as afternoons and evenings were often more difficult for people with Lewy Body. Martin pulled the car over to the side of the road just before turning in to the property, so that his mother would have a view of the river.

"Look, Elizabeth," John said, leaning across the seat and pointing out the window on Elizabeth's side. "Isn't this an amazing view? You will be able to see this from your room."

The facility director, Mrs. Anderson, met them at the door, followed by two aides, one pushing a cart for transferring Elizabeth's personal belongings to her room.

"Mr. Abbott, it's so good to see you again," said Mrs. Anderson with a radiant smile. "And this must be Mrs. Abbott." She knelt down beside Elizabeth's wheelchair. Elizabeth looked at her eyes, and then turned her head to find John's, her eyebrows pulling together into a worried look. John hurried to her side.

"Elizabeth, this is Mrs. Anderson, the woman I met with last week. She is in charge here at Sunset Park, where you will be staying." John touched Elizabeth's hand and kissed her on the cheek. Then he turned to Mrs. Anderson. "Please call me John. And this is Elizabeth."

"Of course," Mrs. Anderson said. "And I'm Kelly. Let's show Elizabeth her room."

The entourage followed Kelly down a hall and around a corner, past a nurses' station to the first door on the left. The room was small, but had a view of the river. John had seen the room the previous week and was so glad it was available.

Once Elizabeth was settled, Martin and James said their goodbyes, promising to return soon. "We'll wait for you in the car, Dad," Martin said as they walked out the door.

Alone with Elizabeth in this place that would surely be her final home, John was again flooded with guilt. Elizabeth hadn't said a word since they arrived, and had barely turned her head to look at him, preferring instead the view from her windows. Finally, John held her head in his hands and gently lifted her face to his and kissed her goodbye. Her lips no longer responded the way they once had, and he barely made it out the door before bursting into tears.

After stopping at Tug's—the casual bar and grill in Harbor Town—for lunch, Martin and James dropped John off at his empty house mid-afternoon. Walking into Elizabeth's study, he could still feel her presence there. It wasn't any easier in the kitchen, which was filled with memories of meals shared together. And when he finally walked into the bedroom they had shared for almost four decades, it was more than he could bear. He crumpled onto the bed and wept until he fell asleep.

Kelly Anderson had told him that things would get better with time, and in a way, they did. His daily visits with Elizabeth became easier to bear. She often lit up when he walked into her room, but soon it became obvious that she was responding as much to the fresh cut flowers he had brought from their garden back home as to his presence. She would reach for them and make sounds to indicate her pleasure as she drew them to her nose and took in their fragrance.

John visited faithfully—if not daily—for several months. His guilt was assuaged as he witnessed Elizabeth's decline, realizing that he would not have been able to care for her this well at home. Once she no longer seemed to recognize him, John's dreadful loneliness set in. Friends tried to engage him in social activities, and Martin often called to ask him to join him for drinks and supper. But none of this eased his pain.

One day he was signing in at the front desk at Sunset Park when he noticed the name of another visitor on the same page of the registry. Mary Margaret Richardson. And the name of the resident she was visiting, Walker Richardson. He stood for a few minutes, staring at the names. His face must have registered his shock because the receptionist, Deborah, asked, "Is something wrong, Mr. Abbott?"

Looking up from the names he had just read, he said, "No. Or maybe. I'm not sure. Do you have a resident here named Walker Richardson?"

"We're really not supposed to give out that sort of information, which seems kind of silly since the visitor sign-in sheets are right there for anyone to see. And yes, Mr. Richardson is a resident here. In fact, his room is just down the hall from your wife's."

John's pulse quickened and he felt faint. Deborah noticed and came out from behind the glass partition between the lobby and her desk and put her hand on his shoulder.

"Are you sure you're okay? Why don't we sit down over here for a minute?" Deborah guided him to a nearby couch and sat with him. He felt dizzy and asked for a glass of water. When she returned with the water, he drank it in big gulps, as though his thirst was unquenchable. He closed his eyes and the name *Mary Margaret Richardson* scrolled across the darkness of his closed eyelids. He opened his eyes and asked, "Is his wife—is Mrs. Richardson—visiting with him today?"

"Yes, I saw her sign in just a few minutes before you got here this morning. Why? Do you know her?"

Before he could answer, he heard a voice he hadn't heard in over forty years. It was deeper than he remembered, but there was no denying its source. "Deborah, I'm sorry to bother you, but Walker needs help, and I couldn't find an aide and—" She stopped when she saw John sitting next to Deborah on the couch.

John stood quickly, with Deborah holding his arm for support. "Be careful, Mr. Abbott. You might still be dizzy."

Mary Margaret stared at him and said, slowly, "Mr. Abbott?" And then, when he didn't answer, she said, "John? Oh, my gosh, is that you?

John nodded, trying to find his voice. His smile came first, and then his answer. "Yes. Mary Margaret? Is that really you?"

She laughed as she caught her breath. "Last time I checked!" That same wonderful sense of humor, still intact after all these years. But then she remembered Walker, and turned to Deborah. "Oh, Deborah, I almost forgot, can you please page someone to Walker's room. He needs help with . . ." She looked at John awkwardly and then back at Deborah ". . . you know, with personal hygiene."

"Of course, Mrs. Richardson." Deborah headed back behind the glass partition, leaving John and Mary Margaret alone.

Mary Margaret spoke first. "What on earth are you doing here, John?"

"I'm visiting my wife. We moved her in here a few months ago. She has Lewy Body Disorder. You?"

Mary Margaret took a moment to steady herself. "Walker . . . Walker has been here for over a year. He has Alzheimer's."

"The receptionist said his room is just down the hall from Elizabeth's. I wonder why we haven't seen each other here before?"

"It's probably because Walker was just moved to this wing recently," Mary Margaret explained. "Oh, and that reminds me, I really need to go check and be sure someone has come to help him. Will you be here long?"

"Oh, sure. I'm usually here for about an hour, sometimes longer. Elizabeth's room is the first one on the left," John pointed to a hallway, "just past the nurses' station. I'm headed there now. You could stop by later."

"Are you sure she wouldn't mind?"

"Oh, she usually doesn't even recognize me these days."

"I understand." Mary Margaret's expression showed that she shared John's sadness over these destructive diseases. "I'll stop by in a little while."

John watched as she walked out of the lobby and headed down the hall. Her gait was a little slower and she no longer had a bouncy ponytail, but her hips still had that sway, and her figure. He didn't need to be thinking about that. *Elizabeth.*

He headed into her room, where he found her in her favorite spot. Her wheelchair was turned towards the windows. Martins were flying in and out of the tall bird houses on the front of the property. Far beyond the lawn, another barge was making its way south on the river. He leaned down to kiss Elizabeth on the cheek, wondering if she would pull away as she often did, but this time he could have sworn he saw a tiny turn at the corners of her mouth. He pulled up a chair and sat next to her and spoke quietly and slowly, telling her small things about his day. He used to tell her about the grandchildren, but she didn't seem to know who they were anymore, and he didn't want to frustrate her. It had become increasingly difficult to find anything to talk about. Just when he was running out of ideas, Mary Margaret knocked on the door.

"May I come in?"

John stood and turned to look at her. It was as if he needed to see her again to believe she was real. "Oh yes, sure. We were just looking at the birds and the river. Come join us."

Mary Margaret walked over and stood by the windows where Elizabeth could see her. John touched Elizabeth's hand and said, "Elizabeth, sweetheart, this is Mary Margaret Richardson, an old friend from college."

Elizabeth looked at Mary Margaret without changing her expression. Then she turned her gaze back to the birds outside the window.

"Elizabeth and I met a number of years ago," Mary Margaret said to John. "At Hutchison. I was teaching there, and Elizabeth came and spoke at assembly once."

"Oh, yes, I remember she told me about that," John said. "Can you believe we both lived in Memphis all these years and never ran into each other?"

"I guess we traveled in different circles. I'd love to catch up sometime. Would you like to have lunch one day? I usually visit Walker in the mornings. My writing group meets for lunch today, but I could do tomorrow."

"That would be great. Shall we just meet in the lobby here, around noon tomorrow?"

"Sounds good. I'm so glad to see you, John."

After Mary Margaret left the room, John turned back to Elizabeth. She had closed her eyes and seemed to be asleep. "Elizabeth?" he leaned closer to her. She opened her eyes and looked straight at him. "I'm leaving now, but I'll be back tomorrow. I love you." When he leaned down to kiss her on the cheek, she turned her face back to the windows.

The novelist works neither to correct nor to condone, not at all to comfort,
but to make what's told alive.

—**Eudora Welty,** *On Writing*

CHAPTER 11

Harbor Town (2015-2017)

Adele could barely speak after listening to John and Mary Margaret's stories. Her mouth hung open as she stared at both of them. The sun cast its late afternoon rays across the patterned rug in their living room and reflected off the empty wine glasses on the coffee table. The room was silent. Finally, she found her voice. "I—I don't know what to say. What both of you have been through is heartbreaking."

John and Mary Margaret looked at each other pensively. John spoke first. "Yes, it has been . . . and it still is."

"You didn't know you were signing up to hear such an epic family saga, did you?" Mary Margaret laughed as she began to gather the empty wine glasses.

"Here, let me help you." Adele moved to help when John stood and stopped her. "Oh, no, you are our guest. I'll get this." He picked up the wine bottle and other items and followed Mary Margaret into the kitchen. "But you're welcome to join us in here," he called out over his shoulder.

"I'll be there in a minute," Adele answered, taking another bit of time to admire the view from their living room window. And then she noticed a group of photographs on the wall behind where she had been sitting. All the pictures were of Mary Margaret's family. A large portrait of her with Walker and their girls. As she scanned the other walls, she realized that there were no pictures of John and his family anywhere, or any pictures of Mary Margaret with John. She looked at her watch—it was almost five—and she wondered if she should go home and let John and Mary Margaret get back to their own lives. But oh—those lives! She wanted to hear more. But first she needed to find the bathroom. And she was curious about the view from upstairs.

"Okay if I go upstairs and look at the view?" she called to the kitchen.

"Oh, sure, make yourself at home," Mary Margaret answered.

As she walked down a hallway at the top of the stairs, she passed a beautiful bedroom. Its pink and pale green flowery curtains and antique four-poster bed beckoned her inside. Everywhere she looked there were bookshelves filled to overflowing with books. A small writing desk was set by the windows with a laptop computer and stacks of printed manuscript pages. Everything about the room was feminine. The room opened out onto the balcony. And yes, the view of the river was magnificent. It was cloudy, which made for a beautiful sunset with pinks and golds reflecting off the water.

Back out in the hallway she found another bedroom and again, looked inside. This one was filled with dark wooden pieces, including a large desk on which sat stacks of paperwork and a wooden gavel. A large leather chair and ottoman commanded one corner of the room. The windows weren't adorned with curtains at all, but were fitted out with wooden indoor shutters. A pair of man's slippers peeked out from under the edge of the bed. Feeling embarrassed, she quickly left the room. Finally, she returned to the kitchen, where Mary Margaret and John were looking at a menu.

"We were thinking of ordering pizza. Will you stay and join us?" Mary Margaret asked.

"Oh, my. I feel like such an intruder, but I have to say that I'm anxious to hear what happened next. I love how the two of you found each other again. I love your house."

"It's Mary Margaret's house," John said.

"Oh, I'm sorry. I just assumed—"

"No worries. The house is just another part of our story," Mary Margaret said.

"And, what about Walker and Elizabeth? Where do they fit into the story now?"

"Well, now you know why we came to hear you talk about Alzheimer's at the book club this morning," John said.

"Yes, that makes sense now. Although I think my journey with my mother and her Alzheimer's was very different from both of yours. Especially yours, John. Lewy Body Disorder has its own set of challenges, doesn't it?"

John nodded.

"And even though Walker has Alzheimer's, I can't imagine that journey with your spouse, Mary Margaret, and how much harder that would be than with an elderly parent."

"It's awful," Mary Margaret said. "And our journeys aren't over yet."

John looked away for a minute as though gathering his thoughts. Finally, he said, "Why don't we sit here in the kitchen for a change of scenery while we wait on the pizza to arrive?"

"Of course, that's fine," Adele said. "I'm eager to hear the rest of your story."

After their morning visits with Elizabeth and Walker the next day, John and Mary Margaret met in the lobby at Sunset Park, as they had agreed. Except for yesterday, they hadn't seen each other in over thirty years.

"Do you know of any good places to have lunch near here?" John asked.

"Sure, there are lots of good places, but—oh, I guess I haven't told you—I, well really *we,* Walker and I bought a house in Harbor Town a few years ago when he retired. We enjoyed the neighborhood together for a while, until he got worse and needed more care than I could provide at home. We chose the neighborhood because it's just down the street from Sunset Park."

"I understand. Same thing happened with Elizabeth. I retired to stay home with her, and I hired help and everything, but it just wasn't enough. Do you ever get over the feelings of guilt?"

Looking around at the other visitors and staff coming and going in the lobby, Mary Margaret said, "Why don't we go to my house for lunch? It will be quieter than a restaurant."

Memories flooded John as he listened to her invitation—memories of the day so many years ago when Elizabeth had invited him to her house for coffee.

"That sounds great, if it isn't too much trouble."

"Not at all. Just follow me. It's just down Island Drive, and then onto River Park Drive."

John had another flashback as he pulled up in front of Mary Margaret's house a few minutes later. He remembered his discomfort the first time he visited her at the Tri Delt house at Ole Miss, almost fifty years ago. Once inside the house, his nerves settled a bit, but not his heart. As they sat at her kitchen table eating chicken salad, the conversation flowed easily. They took turns sharing stories of their marriages, their careers, and their children. They talked for over an hour before Mary Margaret asked, "Would you like to sit in the den where it's more comfortable?"

Comfortable? John's heart was racing. "Sure." As he followed her into the den, he pictured her once again at the Tri Delt house, coming down the stairs for their date to the football game. Her beautiful long hair bouncing off her shoulders. Dancing with her at the jazz club later that night, her skin so soft against his cheek. Sitting in his car, kissing her.

As she turned to sit in a nearby chair, he stopped her. Catching her by the arm with one hand and reaching for her shoulder with the other, he turned her to face him. Her hair was still beautiful, streaked with silver and cut in fashionable layers. Her eyes still sparkled. And those lips—he lifted her chin, and the years disappeared as he kissed her again. She fell into his arms, returning the kiss as he pulled her closer. Mary Margaret pulled away.

"Oh, John, we can't!"

"I know. But—" He pulled her to himself again, and again she didn't fight it. The kiss sent them onto the couch before either would stop. This time it was John. Sitting up straight on the edge of the couch, and then moving to a nearby chair, he took a minute before he spoke.

"You are right. We can't do this. Elizabeth and Walker are right down the street. And despite the fact that I never stopped loving you, I also love her. Does that make sense?"

Mary Margaret touched her lips with the fingers of one hand, as though to contain the kiss, keeping her eyes closed. When she opened them, the reality of their situation rushed back.

"Of course it makes sense, John."

"So, did you stop? Loving me, I mean?"

She shook her head. "Of course not. But like you, I made a life for myself. And Walker is a good man, but—"

"But, what?"

"I'm not sure I was ever in love with him. Marrying Walker was what my family—what society—expected of me."

"How could you live like that for so many years?"

"Not everyone gets to live happily ever after, John. Sometimes we make the best of what we have, and I had a wonderful career teaching school, and we raised two wonderful daughters."

"Didn't you ever stop to wonder if it was enough?" he asked.

"Sometimes, like when I would see your picture in the newspaper, and of course that time when Elizabeth came to Hutchison to speak. She's gorgeous, and what an amazing woman, John." Mary Margaret stared down at her hands, clasped together in her lap "Are you . . . in love with her?"

"Yes. From the first day I met her in the library at Ole Miss. It was my second year of law school and her first year of grad school. We had an instant connection. And a shared history, even at that point in our young lives. She was at Jackson State during the riots there. And, of course, you know about my involvement in the BSU and the protests when we were in school. But with Elizabeth, we were on the same side."

"That's not fair." Mary Margaret stood and crossed her arms. "You know I was on your side with everything that happened at Ole Miss, John. And when we decided not to keep seeing each other, that was mutual."

"I know, but no matter how much we wanted it to work, no matter how much you might have tried to change so you could be with me, there was something you could never be. You could never be Black. And I could never be White."

They sat quietly with those words for a few minutes before John spoke again. "I'm sorry, but I really need to leave. I've got an appointment downtown. Maybe we can visit more another day?"

Mary Margaret nodded, her face lined with tears. John stood and took her face in his hands. But this time he didn't kiss her. He simply wiped her tears with his fingers, and then pulled her in for a hug. It was an embrace neither of them wanted to end.

They saw each frequently at Sunset Park in the coming weeks and months, but agreed to keep their visits short, and always in the lobby at the nursing home. One day, when Mary Margaret was walking down the hall to Walker's room, she noticed a group of people just outside Elizabeth's room. Two young men, one young woman, and two small children were huddled. The men were crying, and one of them was being comforted by the woman. Mary Margaret stopped and introduced herself and asked about Elizabeth.

"She's our mom," one of the young men said. "She just died. Did you know her?"

"Yes. My husband is just down the hall, and I have visited with Elizabeth many times. And with your father. You must be Martin?"

"Oh, I'm James. This is Martin, my brother." The other young man nodded.

"I'm Mary Margaret Richardson. I knew your father years ago when we were at Ole Miss. Is he in with Elizabeth now?"

James nodded. "Please, I'm sure he would be glad to see you."

"Oh, I wouldn't want to intrude on such a private moment. I assume that's why you are all out here in the hall."

"We were just with her, but the funeral home people are coming soon, and we want to take the children back home before they get here." James indicated the young girl and boy standing near their mother, wiping their tears and burying their faces in her dress.

Mary Margaret wasn't sure if she wanted to see John with Elizabeth as he was telling her goodbye, but his sons insisted. She walked into the room to find John sitting on the other side of her bed, holding her left hand in both his hands and crying. It broke her heart for more than the obvious reason. His love for Elizabeth—and the years they spent together—was something she wished she could have had.

John looked up at her, left Elizabeth's side, and crossed the room, taking her in an embrace. She could feel his grief as tears wracked his body.

Several weeks after the funeral, Mary Margaret's phone rang late one night. It startled her, as none of her friends or children ever called past nine or so.

"It's John. Sorry to call so late."

"Oh, John. It's fine. I'm sorry I haven't called. I haven't known whether or not I should. How are you?"

"As good as can be expected, I guess. Not much time to think about how I am, what with all the arrangements for the funeral and everything."

"I can only imagine."

"How's Walker?"

"About the same, thank you. Well, except that he doesn't seem to know who I am at all anymore, which is a mixed blessing."

"How do you mean?"

"Well, I guess I don't feel as much guilt about not having him here at home with me. He seems happy in his own little world at Sunset Park. Sometimes I think he likes the aides there better than me—he sure smiles at them more."

"I'm sure that's just because they are with him all the time. Don't beat up on yourself, Mary Margaret. You are doing everything you can for him."

"Thanks for that, John. So, would you like to come for a visit sometime? I bet you could use a home-cooked meal."

John and Mary Margaret fell into an easy companionship as the months went by. He even went with her to visit Walker some days, and they would have lunch or even take in a movie together. Finally, it was Mary Margaret who made the suggestion.

"John, why don't you sell that big old house and move in with me. You could have the bedroom down the hall from mine. I think you would enjoy Harbor Town. You might even like my book club."

"Well, I'm not sure about the book club, but the invitation to share your home sounds good. And I could help with expenses. I know what Sunset Park is costing you."

"Oh, John, that would be wonderful."

John moved in with Mary Margaret and was gradually welcomed into her social circles in their small community. Even her book club. He was really looking forward to their meeting the month they were reading *Sing, Unburied, Sing* by Mississippi author Jesmyn Ward. He hoped that the group's discussion of the book, which included the legacy of slavery and poverty in the rural South, would be educational for everyone.

Gradually, Mary Margaret's life with Walker intensified as he got sick with pneumonia and had to be hospitalized. He began to eat less, which often happens with Alzheimer's patients. After Walker spent several days in the hospital, the doctor told Mary Margaret that she had a difficult decision to make: Walker might die if they didn't insert a feeding tube into his stomach, through which he would receive his only nourishment. This would require surgery, but without it, Walker would probably slowly starve to death.

Mary Margaret discussed the difficult choice with her daughters, and finally they all agreed that they didn't want him to suffer a painful death. And his quality of life at Sunset Park was pretty good, all things considered. Most days he appeared happy and wasn't in physical pain. So, she consented to have the tube inserted.

Because Walker's mental state precluded him from understanding what was happening, he would occasionally pull the tube loose, which required a return trip to the hospital. The nurses at Sunset Park kept the feeding tube site covered with a large bandage, and tried dressing Walker in pullover shirts that he couldn't unbutton in front, which helped most of the time.

John was always there for Mary Margaret during these stressful times with Walker. As painful as it was for him to return to Sunset Park, he often went with her on her visits. And when she would get depressed, he would take her somewhere to cheer her up, like the ballet or a show at the Orpheum Theater, or in nice weather, for a walk through the Botanic Gardens or the Memphis Zoo. And when they returned to Mary Margaret's house in Harbor Town, they settled into a comfortable relationship, cooking meals together, reading together, and sleeping in their separate bedrooms. There were times, of course, when they wanted to share Mary Margaret's bed, but her loyalty to Walker and their sense of morality won out.

"Well, that explains a lot," Adele said, thinking about the bedrooms she had discovered upstairs earlier. "I am truly blown away by your story. I remember when you asked me about someone to help you, Mary Margaret, like an eldercare specialist. I really don't know anyone like that, but I can look into it, if you'd like me to."

"You know," Mary Margaret said, looking at John and then back at Adele, "talking with you makes me realize I don't need any additional help. John, my girls, and the wonderful people at Sunset Park are really a terrific support group. I only need someone to hear my story—our story. And that someone is you. Your interest has been such a gift to us, Adele."

She looked at John, and they both nodded at Adele as Mary Margaret added, "Really, a type of saving grace. Do you mind if I hug you?"

"Of course not." Adele and Mary Margaret both stood and embraced. As their hug ended, Adele left her arms on Mary Margaret's shoulders, looked into her eyes, and said, "I am honored. You know, some people are afraid to share their stories with me, since I'm an author. They are scared I'm going to write about them."

They all laughed. John stood and put his arm around Mary Margaret, facing Adele. "Well, you'll have to beat Mary Margaret to it. She's been spending lots of time on her laptop lately."

"Yes, and I only wish I had started writing when I was young. Remember when I told you about my friendship with Eudora Welty when I was a teenager back in Jackson? I was still teaching school full time when she died in 2001. Between teaching and raising two girls, I never stopped long enough to consider writing a book. Until now."

It had been a long day. Before Adele left, they talked about getting together again soon. She really wanted to know where life would take them next. Adele finally said her goodbyes and walked home, leaving John and Mary Margaret to continue their journey.

All literature is protest.

—Richard Wright

CHAPTER 12

John and Mary Margaret (2017-2019)

The month after Adele's visit to the Harbor Town book club, Mary Margaret and John hosted the meeting. The book they discussed was *Before We Were Yours* by Lisa Wingate, a wrenching novel based on the true story of the children who were kidnapped, abused, and sold by Georgia Tann at the Tennessee Children's Home Society orphanage in Memphis between 1939 and 1950.

"Elizabeth would have loved this book," John said, after everyone left at the end of the evening.

"How so?" Mary Margaret asked.

"Because she spent her career—forty years—working with children from poor home situations. And it was her greatest joy to see them thrive during their time at Sarah's Place. And to help them find good adoptive parents."

"Oh, yes, I remember when she talked about that during assembly at Hutchison. It seemed that most of the children were Black, right?"

John nodded. "Most, but not all. That's what's so interesting about this story that happened with the orphanage in Memphis. All of those children were White, but they were treated like slaves—like they were owned by Georgia Tann. And even though the White people who adopted them might have been well-meaning, it amounted to buying those children."

Mary Margaret let John's words take her mind to the plantation home where her college roommate, Shannon, grew up in the Mississippi Delta. Mary Margaret had gone home with Shannon to visit her family one weekend during their sophomore year. And although Shannon had told her that it had been two generations since enslaved people had worked there, Mary Margaret felt uncomfortable in the house. It was as if the ghosts of those slaves haunted the place. One night after dinner, Mary Margaret had asked Shannon about Abigail, the elderly Black maid wearing a uniform with a white apron who had served them.

"So, how long has Abigail worked for your family?"

"Since before I was born. I don't ever remember her not being at our house."

"But she's an employee, right?"

"Of course. And we've always treated her like family."

"What about her family? Were her parents slaves?"

"Not her parents, but her grandparents were. My great-grandfather freed them after the Civil War."

"Mary Margaret?" John interrupted her thoughts.

"Huh? Oh, sorry. I was just remembering something from a long time ago."

"What was it?"

"You remember my roommate our freshman year, Shannon?"

John nodded.

"Well, she grew up on a plantation in the Mississippi Delta, and her great-grandfather owned slaves. It felt kind of creepy when I went home with her for a weekend once. I was just remembering that, and thinking about those children Georgia Tann kidnapped and sold in

Memphis. Hard to believe that was still happening when we were born."

John and Mary Margaret spent many days reading, and discussing books and history, race and politics. Mary Margaret felt like she had only been taught one side of history growing up White in Jackson. She had tried to give her daughters a more complete view of things, and she was relieved when they both accepted her relationship with John.

"I think it's great, Mom," Claire had said on one of her phone calls from New York. "It's about time people down South were more open to biracial relationships." And John's sons, who had met Mary Margaret at the nursing home the day their mother died, had also welcomed her into their family, although it wasn't official.

Walker's Alzheimer's was getting worse, and he was deteriorating. The doctor at Sunset Park had told Mary Margaret that he could live quite a few more years, unless he had a major medical event unrelated to the Alzheimer's. But that event came during a crisp weekend in October of 2018. Claire had flown down from New York and Emily had driven up from Oxford to spend some time with their mother and John, and to see their father. It was serendipitous that they were both there when the phone rang on Friday morning with news that Walker had suffered a heart attack.

"Is it Dad?" Emily asked as Margaret was hanging up the phone.

"Yes, honey."

The four of them climbed into the car and headed over to Sunset Park. As they stood around Walker's bed, Mary Margaret was surprised by what she felt. Her daughters put their arms around her among a torrent of tears. Mary Margaret had watched John's grief when Elizabeth died, and she knew this was something different. Walker had essentially been gone for several years now, and this didn't feel like sadness. It felt like relief, compounded by guilt at having those feelings. John and Mary Margaret spent the next couple of months settling Walker's affairs and getting used to having more time together, without the constraints of daily visits to Sunset Park.

Christmas came quickly, and Mary Margaret and John decided to spend the day with James Abbott and his family in Oxford. They got there early enough to open gifts with their grandchildren who had adopted Mary Margaret and affectionately called her "May-May." After a scrumptious meal, John and Mary Margaret took a walk to the Ole Miss campus, which was just a few blocks from James' house. Memories sprouted as they walked past the Tri Delt House, and then into the Grove where they had ended their youthful relationship. They stopped under a tree that could have been one that covered them with shade as they had sat and studied on a blanket together. It might have been where they had discussed Faulkner.

"Remember this?" John asked, putting his arm around Mary Margaret in the chilly breeze.

"Of course. Lots of happy times here, but also the end of that happiness." Her voice sounded bittersweet.

"I think it's a great place for beginnings," John said, moving in front of Mary Margaret. "If I was fifty years younger, I would get down on my knee, but you know how much I hurt that knee playing football."

"What? Of course you can't . . . wait . . . what are you doing?"

John reached into his pocket and held a small box which he opened, revealing a beautiful diamond ring. Taking Mary Margaret's hand in his, he asked, "Will you marry me?"

Maybe she moved a little more slowly than she would have fifty years earlier, but Mary Margaret didn't lose much time grabbing that ring, putting it on her finger, and throwing her arms around John. "Oh, John, yes. A thousand times, yes!"

It was only fitting that John and Mary Margaret would be married in Oxford, where their relationship began back in 1966. And although John and Elizabeth had also married there, back in 1973, John's thoughts were totally on Mary Margaret when she walked down the aisle in the Faulkner Room at The Jefferson—a beautiful venue on a lake just seven miles east of the Ole Miss campus.

Mary Margaret looked much younger than her seventy years in her beautiful champagne lace tea-length dress with a high-low hem and three-quarter-length sleeves, also lace. John was as handsome as ever in a cutaway black tuxedo jacket with hickory-striped tuxedo pants and a platinum satin vest, topped off with a platinum tapestry ascot.

Mary Margaret's daughters and John's sons served as attendants, along with their grandchildren. It was storybook perfect, albeit a bit untraditional, especially for Mississippi. After the reception and a grand send-off with sparklers out by the lake, Mr. and Mrs. John Abbott headed back into town for a honeymoon spent in the Governor's Suite at Chancellor's House, an elegant boutique hotel near the square. Surrounded by Southern grandeur wherever they looked, John and Mary Margaret were treated like royalty—quite a different reception than the one they had received when they went anywhere together in Oxford fifty years earlier.

Sitting on the balcony of their suite, drinking mimosas the next morning, John teased Mary Margaret. "Well, was it worth the wait?"

They both laughed, and Mary Margaret—ever the Southern belle—blushed. "I think we did pretty well for two old people."

"Does this mean I get to move into your bedroom when we get home?"

"Well, that depends. Where am I going to write? A woman needs a room of her own, you know."

"I've been thinking about that." John put his mimosa down on the table by their chairs and stood, looking down the street towards the square. "What if we move to a new place—one that has a master bedroom suite and two studies, one for each of us?"

Mary Margaret wondered if it bothered John to be living in a house that had belonged to Walker. And how it might feel for him to move into the bedroom she and Walker had shared. But she couldn't imagine giving up their view of the river.

"Oh, my. You continue to be full of surprises. There's a realtor in Harbor Town—I know her from yoga. I could ask her if there are any other houses on the river that would have a floor plan like that."

"Harbor Town?" John looked at Mary Margaret with a mischievous smile. "I was thinking about Oxford."

Mary Margaret pulled away from John, her face registering her surprise. "Really?"

"Well, there's not really any reason to stay in Memphis now, is there? Both Emily and James are teaching at Ole Miss, and James' family is here. Wouldn't it be great to be near two of our kids and our grandkids?"

Mary Margaret's head was spinning. This wasn't something she had anticipated, but John had obviously given it some thought. She would be leaving her writing group in Harbor Town, but she would be living in Oxford, Mississippi. She could imagine herself sitting up on the balcony at Square Books, reading and writing for hours. What if she actually finished that book she was writing? What if one day she would see it in the front window of the bookstore, or even be doing a book signing? Her imagination spiraled when John brought her back to earth.

"And—"

"And?" Mary Margaret interrupted him. "You mean there's more? How long have you been cooking up this plan?"

"Well, I was thinking that I would need something to do while you're working on that bestseller. I got a call recently from someone at the law school—actually, they've been after me since I retired in Memphis—with an invitation to be an adjunct professor there. It would only be part-time, which would mean plenty of time for you to write, but also time to spend together and with the kids. What do you think?"

"This is a lot to take in, John. Do you realize that in the past five months I've become a widow and a newlywed, and now I would be moving to a new town?"

"Yes. And with no excuses not to finish writing that novel. Or several novels." John put his arms around Mary Margaret and pulled her in for a long embrace. It didn't take long for them to find each other's lips, and then to head back inside their honeymoon suite.

Mary Margaret's house on the river sold quickly. She and John found the perfect home in Oxford, right on South Lamar, just a few blocks from Square Books and a nice walk or short drive to campus. They moved in late summer, when the magnolias were in full bloom in their new front yard. The house was a Victorian treasure, with a wrap-around front porch where they could enjoy their morning coffee or a late afternoon cocktail while watching the people on the sidewalk or going by in cars. Mary Margaret found people-watching to be helpful in her writing, as she imagined the lives of the characters passing by. Sometimes she would catch the eye of a pedestrian and wave, hoping they would walk up to the porch for a visit. And the best times were when James and his family would stroll by and the grandkids would come running up the steps and into their arms. Or when Ellen would call and say, "Hey Mom, I'm on the square. Want to meet me for coffee at Uptown?" Their coffee visits would last for hours sometimes, as they discussed Emily's classes and the progress on Mary Margaret's book.

The fall semester brought memories of their freshman year fifty years ago. Mary Margaret loved to stroll through campus, watching the students coming and going from classes and relaxing in the Grove with their friends. She had read that there were almost 3,000 Black students enrolled at Ole Miss for the 2019-2020 academic year, and it was refreshing to see so many of them on campus.

John was happy to learn that a Black woman had been elected student body president in 2012, but then she had gone on to Texas for law school. He only wished she had stayed at Ole Miss. There were sixty-seven Black students enrolled in the law school in the fall of 2019, out of a total of 412 students. He was enjoying teaching, and the students seemed to appreciate his years of experience in Memphis. And they were excited to learn that he was one of the students who were arrested for protesting at Fulton Chapel back in 1970, and that he had been a leader in the BSU.

"What was it like back then, Judge Abbott?" The young Black man asking the question was a first-year law student from Memphis.

John smiled and took a deep breath. "Well, we were either bullied or we weren't seen at all. I'm not sure which was worse."

"Why did you choose to come back here now, after the way you were treated then?" another student asked.

"Yeah," another student added, "and why did you choose to stay here for law school?"

John put his lecture notes down, walked around in front of his desk and sat on the edge of it. He looked at the room full of eager faces, and he chose his words carefully.

"I stayed because I didn't want to give up on Mississippi. We can't accomplish anything by running away from our battles. I guess I had a love-hate relationship with Ole Miss, but eventually the love won out."

A White female student on the front row raised her hand. John nodded at her, and she spoke, her voice quiet and her expression tentative: "Did it have anything to do with a certain White girl you met your freshman year?" She appeared relieved when he laughed at her question.

"Now where did you hear about that?" he smiled at the student as he asked.

"Well, I took a class from Emily Richardson last year. She told me about her mother—about your wife, Mary Margaret."

John walked back around behind his desk and picked up his lecture notes. "That's definitely a story for another time and place." And then he looked at the student who had asked the question and added, "but it's a damn good story."

I refuse to accept the view that mankind is so tragically bound to the starless midnight of racism and war that the bright daybreak of peace and brotherhood can never become a reality. . . . I believe that unarmed truth and unconditional love will have the final word.

—Martin Luther King, Jr.

EPILOGUE

Ole Miss (2020)

A few months later, in January of 2020, John received a call from a visiting professor in Southern Studies, inviting him to speak at an event being planned for February 25, the fiftieth anniversary of the protests at Fulton Chapel.

"It will be a two-day event," the professor said, "with a film screening and panel discussion on the twenty-fourth and a ceremony at Fulton Chapel on the twenty-fifth, followed by a Black History keynote address at the Student Union."

"That sounds amazing. Who else will be there?" John asked.

"So far, five of the eight students who were expelled are coming, along with a few others."

John's mind raced back to that day, to the courage Dianna showed, and the persistence Eddie demonstrated. It would be wonderful to be with them again, even if the memories might be painful. John went home and discussed the event with Mary Margaret that evening.

"Oh, John, I think that would be wonderful," Mary Margaret said, pouring them both a glass of wine and stirring a pot of chicken soup on the stove. January had brought a deep chill with it, even in Mississippi, so they chose the warmth of their kitchen over the front porch. "What do they want you to do?"

He told her about the agenda for the two-day event, and she was enthusiastic, as she always was when it came to important events in John's life.

"I'm sure James and his family will want to be there, and Martin will drive down from Memphis. And of course Emily will come. Maybe Claire can even fly down from New York. It would be wonderful to have all our children and grandchildren together."

February 24 came quickly, and John joined the other honored guests for the film screening and panel discussion. Martin and Claire arrived the next morning, and by noon the home was full of family. Mary Margaret had cooked for days, and the dining room table was full for the first time since they moved in.

Martin stood and raised his wine glass towards his father. "A toast to Judge Abbott!" Everyone joined him, raising their glasses and adding their accolades.

"To the Ole Miss Eight!" came from Emily.

"To the future!" James said.

"And to more progress for Mississippi!" Claire added.

Everyone looked at Mary Margaret, who took a minute to find her voice. When she spoke, it was with tears in her eyes. "To love."

After lunch they arrived on the campus and headed to Fulton Chapel. John found Eddie and Dianna, and they all shared embraces and tears. They visited for about thirty minutes, not nearly enough time to catch up on a half century of life. Finally, it was time for the ceremony, which began at three.

Several Black people spoke about how they had been treated at Ole Miss in 1970, treatment that included receiving a constant barrage of racial slurs, having hot water thrown on them, and living in constant fear. One person described his experience as "not feeling human." Another spoke about his anger at being ignored, and how that was what had fueled his participation in the protest. Even in the midst of the sharing of such intense and emotional stories, there was also joking and a celebration of their kinship—their brotherhood in the fight against injustice.

Eddie talked about how his love for Ole Miss survived. He had only recently retired from his dream career—teaching at the university for over forty years.

John surprised Mary Margaret by telling about the harassment he received from White students when the two of them tried to have a relationship during their freshman year. And when he told about how they found each other again, forty-three years later, and were now married, the crowd burst into applause.

But John's favorite part of the ceremony was when his old friend Dianna, who had already earned all the credits required for graduation before she was expelled, finally received her diploma. "I almost didn't come today," she said, tears streaming. "Never thought I would set foot on this campus again. But here I am. Maybe now the healing can begin."

The ceremony was followed by a Black History Month keynote address at six at the Student Union. John looked around the building—which had been remodeled in 2019—remembering the afternoon he and Eddie had stood on the tables quoting Fannie Lou Hamer, dancing to Eldridge Cleaver's cry for Black Power as they played "Soul on Wax," and watching Dianna burn a Confederate flag. The building looked completely different now, but the physical renovation could never erase that event from his mind—and hopefully not from the hearts of others who were there that day.

The evening's speaker was Dr. Yusef Salaam. He was one of the Central Park Five, the five young men of color who were arrested, tried, and wrongfully convicted of raping a woman in New York's Central Park in 1989. Dr. Salaam had spent six years and eight months in jail for a crime he didn't commit. Finally, DNA evidence proved his innocence, as well as the innocence of the other four men, who had served as many as thirteen years incarcerated. He spoke about the need for prison reform, and reform of the criminal system of injustice. But he also spoke of the Central Park Five's story as ultimately a love story between God and his people, and their eventual acquittal as a miracle in modern times.

John and Mary Margaret sat together during the keynote holding hands, that simple expression of affection for which they had received so much hatred. They were proud of the social progress that had been made, but they knew that there was still much work to be done. Maybe John's students, and even his and Mary Margaret's children, would be part of ushering in a future marked by love rather than hatred. Maybe, just maybe, he and Mary Margaret would live to see more miracles.

AUTHOR'S NOTE

Every writer, like everybody else, thinks he's living through the crisis of the ages. To write honestly and with all our powers is the least we can do, and the most.

—**Eudora Welty,** *On Writing*

I wrote most of this book while isolated during the Covid-19 virus pandemic in the spring and summer of 2020. And yes, I thought I was "living through the crisis of the ages," as Miss Welty wrote. Parallel to the health crisis was the growing unrest in our country as protests erupted nationwide in response to the killing of unarmed Black men by White police officers. The inequality and mistreatment of Blacks started in the 1500s, when the first enslaved Africans were brought to what would become South Carolina. Now, 500 years later, the descendants of those enslaved—who were legally freed in 1862—are still fighting for justice and equality.

I was born in Jackson, Mississippi, in 1951 and came of age in the 1960s Jim Crow South. I graduated from high school in 1969, with fewer than a dozen Black students in our school of over 1,200. The following year, school busing to achieve integration would change the landscape of our historically segregated education system in Jackson and other parts of the South forever. My first cousin, John Jones, who was a few years behind me at the same high school in Jackson, edited a book that recounts that story: *Lines Were Drawn: Remembering Court-Ordered Integration at a Mississippi High School* (University Press of Mississippi, 2016). But I missed that experience because I left home to enter the University of Mississippi as a freshman in 1969.

While researching the events on the Ole Miss campus in the 1960s, I was surprised to learn about the protest at Fulton Chapel in February of 1970. I asked my husband—who was a college senior when the protest happened—and several other friends who were at Ole Miss at the time, and very few even remember the event. The injustices that were happening to minorities at my school were not even on my personal radar.

In 2018, I edited a collection of essays by twenty-six Southern authors, *Southern Writers on Writing.* During the process of inviting authors to contribute essays, I realized how few Black authors I knew personally. Through connections with other writers, I was introduced to four, including Ralph Eubanks, a Mississippi native, Ole Miss graduate, and visiting professor. His essay in that collection, "The Past is Just Another Name For Today," and his book *Ever is a Long Time: A Journey into Mississippi's Dark Past* were important elements in my awakening to much of my home state's history.

This novel is a work of fiction, but it was inspired by historic times and events. In order to stay true to the social and political climate of each decade in the book, and to capture important elements of the culture in Mississippi and Memphis during the years that John and Mary Margaret's story spans, my research included numerous books and articles—some for historical details and some for inspiration. These are the most important of those resources.

Asim, Jabari. *The N Word: Who Can Say It, Who Shouldn't, and Why* (New York, Houghton Mifflin, 2007)

Blount, Jeffrey. *The Emancipation of Evan Walls* (Virginia Beach, VA, Koehler Books, 2019)

Branston, John. "Battering Ram: The Tragedy of Busing Revisited: A look back at the effect busing had on Memphis' public schools, forty years on." (*Memphis Magazine*, March 4, 2011)

Burns, Trip. "Real Violence: 50 Years Ago at Woolworth." (*Jackson Free Press* May 23, 2013)

Dent, Nigel. "A Question of Repair: Recounting the arrests of 89 black Ole Miss activists in 1970," (*Daily Mississippian* March 2, 2020)

Eubanks, W. Ralph. *Ever is a Long Time: A Journey into Mississippi's Dark Past* (New York, Basic Books, 2003)

Eubanks, W. Ralph. "The Unhealed Wounds of a Mass Arrest of Black Students at Ole Miss, Fifty Years Later." (*The New Yorker*, February 23, 2020)

Horn, Teena F., Alan Huffman, and John Griffin Jones, editors. *Lines Were Drawn: Remembering Court-Ordered Integration at a Mississippi High School* (Jackson, Mississippi, University Press of Mississippi, 2016)

Land, Robert. "Rebel Land: A Racial History of Oxford and Ole Miss." (*Jackson Free Press* December 12, 2012)

Laymon, Kiese. *Heavy: An American Memoir* (New York, Scribner, 2018)

Mayfield, Kenneth Sr. *To Be Born Black in Mississippi: Why I Became a Civil Rights Lawyer* (Kenneth Mayfield, Sr., 2011)

McArthur, Danny. "1970 Fulton Chapel protests commemorated on 50th anniversary." (*Daily Journal* February 25, 2020)

McKenzie, Danny. "The 'other' turning point." (*Daily Journal* February 20, 2005)

After I finished writing this book, I have continued to be inspired by the writings of several Black authors, including the following:

Eubanks, W. Ralph. *The House at the End of the Road: The Story of Three Generations of an Interracial Family in the American South* (Jackson, Mississippi, University Press of Mississippi, 2009)

Glaude, Eddie S., Jr. *Begin Again: James Baldwin's America and Its Urgent Lessons for Our Own* (New York, Crown, 2020)

Gwin, Minrose. *The Queen of Palmyra: A Novel* (New York, Harper Collins, 2010)

Robinson, Marilyn. *Jack* (New York, Farrar, Straus and Giroux, 2020)

Wilkerson, Isabel. *Caste: The Origins of our Discontents* (New York, Random House, 2020)

And now for a word about John Abbott and Mary Margaret Sutherland. They are totally fictional characters. Of course, Mary Margaret's life mirrors my own childhood and coming of age in Jackson, and pledging Delta Delta Delta sorority at Ole Miss in the late 1960s. She and I share lives of White privilege and dreams of becoming writers. But that's where the similarity ends.

The inspiration for John Abbott does come from two historical figures—Don Cole and Kenneth Mayfield—two of the Ole Miss Eight who were arrested and expelled for protesting on campus in February of 1970.

Those of you who have read my short story collection, *Friends of the Library* (Koehler Books, 2019), will recognize Adele, the fictional author who befriends John and Mary Margaret when Adele speaks at their book club. Their story was a favorite among readers of that collection, several of whom suggested that I expand it into a novel. I decided to keep Adele on in the role of a reliable observer-narrator in this book, using her as a fictional device by which John and Mary Margaret share their stories with the reader.

A final word, this time about setting. I have only lived in four places in my life, and this book takes the reader to three of those four: Jackson and Oxford, Mississippi, and Memphis, Tennessee, where I ended up in 1988. In 2021, I've been living in my favorite home since 2014, just a couple of blocks from the Mississippi River in the downtown neighborhood known as Harbor Town. I would be happy to stay here for my "sunset years," and I wish that Sunset Park were a real place.

DISCUSSION QUESTIONS

1. *John and Mary Margaret* has two protagonists, but also two strong supporting characters—Elizabeth and Walker. Did you have a favorite character, and why? If the book is made into a movie, who should play these parts? (Remember that these four characters age from their teen years into their seventies.)

2. How did you feel about Adele's place as a reliable observer-narrator? Did you like the use of her as a connecting *device* between John and Mary Margaret's stories, which spanned nearly seventy years?

3. What did you think about Mary Margaret's friendship with Eudora Welty? Do you think it changed Mary Margaret's understanding of race issues in the South?

4. Like John, his friends Eddie and Dianna were modeled after historic people who were arrested and expelled from Ole Miss because of their participation in the protest at Fulton Chapel in 1970. What did you think about their re-appearing in the Epilogue at the (real, historic) fiftieth anniversary of the event? Did it give some closure for "Dianna" to finally receive her diploma?

5. The settings for the book are all places where the author has lived: Jackson, Mississippi (her birthplace and hometown), Oxford, Mississippi (where she went to school at Ole Miss), and Memphis (where she has lived since 1988). Were the areas of Memphis—the poor and working-class Black neighborhoods, the upper-middle-class Black and White neighborhoods, and the new urban development on the Mississippi River—clearly delineated? Which was your favorite location in the book, and why?

6. Although this is a work of fiction, the author has chosen to use numerous real locations, historic events, and even some historic people. What did you think about the mixing of the historic with the fictional in the book?

7. How informed were you, before reading the book, about the racial protests that happened on the Ole Miss campus in the 1960s and '70s? Or the riots at Jackson State University, in Jackson, Mississippi in 1970? Why do you think these events received less national attention than the riots in Detroit (1967), Los Angeles (1965), Newark (1967), and Kent State University (1970)?

8. Before reading John and Elizabeth's story, had you known about Lewy Body Disorder, and the differences between it and Alzheimer's Disease?

9. If you grew up in the South, how did the desegregation of the schools in the 1970s affect your life? For White readers: did you, or your children, leave the newly segregated public schools to attend private schools, or did you stay in the public schools? Would you make that choice again today, and why? For Black readers, were you or your children involved in forced integration and busing in the South, and if so, how did it affect your or their lives?

10. How did you feel about John and Elizabeth sending their boys to private schools in Memphis? Or about Mary Margaret and Walker sending their girls to a private school? Did it matter to you that the schools their children attended were not established because of segregation?

11. How did John and Elizabeth's marriage, and Mary Margaret and Walker's, affect John and Mary Margaret's relationship when they found each other again fifty years later? Were you glad they had separate bedrooms—and remained "chaste"—before they married?

12. What, if anything, surprised you most in the book, and why?

ACKNOWLEDGMENTS

Writing a book that covers nearly seventy years in three different Southern cities involved a fair amount of research. I have cited references in my Author's Note, and now it's time to thank the people who helped me.

Numerous generous people read an early draft of the manuscript and gave me invaluable feedback on historical and cultural details, as well as the language that was appropriate to those places and times.

For the chapters and scenes set in Memphis, Tennessee: many thanks to Memphians Sarah Hodges, Suzanne Smith Henley, Anne Mathes, and Terre Fratesi Greer. Also to Mary Elizabeth Riddle and Laurie Stanton of Hutchison School. For the chapters and scenes set at the University of Mississippi in Oxford, Mississippi between 1966 and 1970: I am especially thankful to Oxford native Deb Davidson Mashburn and to my Tri Delta sorority sisters Elaine Kimbrough Gray, Corlea Sims Burnett, Pamela Butts Mashburn, and Gayle Gresham Henry. Special thanks to two amazing Black authors I am blessed to call friends: Ralph Eubanks—who is also a native Mississippian, Ole

Miss alum and visiting professor—and Jeffrey Blount, who provided significant feedback.

Other authors who were important early readers include Claire Fullerton and Mandy Haynes. Mandy deserves additional kudos for being the first to suggest that I turn John and Mary Margaret's short story from my collection *Friends of the Library* into a novel.

Many thanks to my team at Koehler Books—John Koehler, Joe Coccaro, Marshall McClure, Kellie Emery, Lauren Sheldon, and Ariana Abud for believing in me and producing such a beautiful book. And to my publicist Kathie Bennett who worked her magic to help *John and Mary Margaret* find its way into the hands of readers everywhere, with much help from devoted booksellers and librarians. I am also eternally grateful to you, the faithful readers and book clubs who have embraced me from the beginning of my writing career and continue to remind me why I write—to share stories, dreams, cultures, ideals, beliefs, and sometimes a different lens through which to view the world.

Finally, I could not have written this book—or any of my previous books—without the support of my husband Bill, who has worked as a physician (Dr. William Cushman) for forty-seven years and as an Orthodox priest (Father Basil) for thirty-four years. His work ethic and love for his dual careers has always inspired me, especially as I began my "late life career" as a published author in 2017, at age sixty-five. We celebrated our fiftieth wedding anniversary in June of 2020, isolating in our home in Memphis in the middle of the Covid-19 pandemic. That same month, my husband retired after forty-three years at the Veterans Administration and started a new job at the University of Tennessee Health Science Center at age seventy-two. *John and Mary Margaret* is a literary love child born of that pivotal summer, and I offer her with great joy to my husband, my family and friends, and to you, my readers.